THE SHORT NIGHT

THE SHORT NIGHT

RUSSELL TURNER

CUTTING EDGE

ISBN-13: 978-1-957868-78-3

Published by
Cutting Edge Books
PO Box 8212
Calabasas, CA 91372
www.cuttingedgebooks.com

CHAPTER ONE

SUPPOSE it started when the plane touched LaGuardia.

It was damn cold for April and I was shivering, but it had little to do with the actual cold. It was crazy, I'd tried not to think of Doris ever since I got Hanns' call that the will was finally settled. But as the big plane circled New York—and at night that's one of the greatest pictures in the world—something, maybe the stewardess, made me think of Doris. The stewardess was a nice blonde kid but she had a habit of chewing her words like Doris did at night when she was switching from wine to rye.

Then for no reason I remembered the first time I took her on the road. That was in the Southern Association and we were in some sweaty little town when that goddamn moon-faced cop came in to the dugout during the the inning and drawled loudly, "There a Lester Dolsan he-ar?"

And when I asked what he wanted, he said, "Boy, you'd better come with me. Got a drunken woman downtown raising all sorts of hell. Claim's she's your wife, boy."

Even now, over the steady drone of the plane's four engines, I could still hear the silence in the dugout, in the whole crummy ball park. Then the few soft snickers. And Mac Lebang, the manager with the beer nose, cursing as I followed the cop, asking me, "We're in the middle of a ball game, Red, or isn't that as important as your rummy broad?"

I busted his red-veined nose and it took me two more seasons before I got back into the Association, or into any form of organized ball.

Then as the plane started the long lazy landing glide that always makes me sweat, I saw the final picture of Doris; her thin body so terribly frail and waxen-looking against the pinkish water of the bath tub ... the cuts on her wrists neat and professional ... the calm care she must have taken with the razor blades.

We came in over Flushing Bay for a smooth landing, taxied over to the main building. I only had slacks and a sport shirt on, and when I stood on the stairs they had run up to the plane door, the cold air hit me like an iced dagger. Alva Hanns was waiting and he shook my hand as we walked into the building, asked, "How's Vero Beach, Red?"

"Hot. We've got some good boys this year."

Alva was not only my lawyer, he was also the one and only Red Dolsan fan, always had been—even when he was Doris' lawyer. He looked me over, said "Les, you remind me of DiMaggio, you dress so differently. You've lost some blubber, must be near your old playing weight."

"Yeah, now if I could only lose about 15 years, I'd try out for first," I said, finding my battered pigskin over-nighter that did me for all these years. I took out a sweat shirt and put it on, then an old ball cap to keep my bald noggin warm.

Alva shook his big grey head. "Well, I suppose you can afford to look like a bum. Got my car outside, give you all the details of the settlement as we drive to town—I only could give you a bare outline over the phone."

We got into his Packard, which seemed a lot like Alva—old, powerful and dignified, and of course he started talking baseball. I told him about the Dodgers and how Pee Wee's legs were holding up, then he asked about Porto Rico and I told him a little of a kid sugar cane hand I'm bringing along, a runty kid who's hard to pitch to and about the greatest bad ball hitter I've ever seen.

Like all old time fans, (and 'fan' is short for fanatic), Alva couldn't keep still. He cut in with, "You never saw a real bad ball hitter if you didn't see Big Ed Delahanty. There was a man who could hit *anything*."

"I remember his name."

"You're not old enough to have heard of him," Alva said smugly. "He played for Washington back in 1900, or 1902. Hell of a batsman. Story is he got drunk one night on a train, stepped off near Niagara Falls, stumbled over an open railroad bridge. They found his drowned body a week later. Red, why do so many ball players hit the bottle?"

"Why limit it to ball players? Why do so many people hide in a bottle? Ball players—maybe the training grind is so damn long and it's the only way they can relax. Look, what happens now with the will?"

"We're having a meeting in my office tomorrow morning at ten. Mrs. Andrews will be there with her lawyer. As I told you over the phone, Doris' estate amounts to a few thousand under a half a million. I've worked out the following settlement: She wants the house on 70th Street, and ..."

"What house?"

Hanns shook his head. "You're certainly the most casual client I ever had. Doris' father left her a town house, which was converted into a small apartment house long before she married you. Pays a handsome profit. Well, the old lady claims she wants that for sentimental reasons. We let her have it but in return she has agreed to pay all inheritance taxes, which certainly will be more than the value of the house. She has also agreed to pay all legal fees. As I told you, you are to receive the income from the principal and upon your death, the fund will go to the old lady, unless you have an heir. Everything considered, and of course you know you're getting a rooking, it's the best I could do."

"You did okay. I suppose the old bitch is sore she can't lay her claws on the ninety-six thousand Doris and I had in the joint bank account."

"Actually, Red, she was astonished that Doris had spent so little of her inheritance."

"She must be over 65 now. What does the old bag want more money for? She sure won't outlive me."

Hanns smiled, showing his strong teeth. "If Mrs. Andrews should be deceased at the time of your death, we agreed that the principal goes to some dog and cat society to which she's leaving her millions."

I thought about it for a moment. "Crazy the way she hates my guts. Hell, I never even saw the old biddy more than once or twice."

"Her reaction is a kind of defense mechanism on her part. Since somebody must be responsible for her only daughter being an alcoholic and a suicide, and since she refuses to see she is to blame, of course, why you become the whipping boy. You know my feelings on the matter. We could have licked her in court—Doris left everything to you and it should be yours, legally, morally, or any other way you want to look at it. But you insisted that …"

"Come off it, Alva, I have all the dough I'll ever need. A court battle would only have dragged Doris' name through the headline mud. Maybe her mother doesn't mind that, but I do." And I wondered if that was the real reason, or was I afraid the notoriety would also lose me my job as a Dodger scout, my last link with the game? "What's this heir angle?"

Alva smiled. "I merely inserted it so it doesn't look as though we're completely throwing in the towel. After all, from the old lady's point of view, you never had a kid with Doris, you're almost 45—she isn't taking much of a chance."

As we crossed the 59th Street Bridge Alva asked, "Still keeping that apartment at the Balton Towers?"

"Yeah."

Alva sighed. "Red, you'll never end up in Cooperstown, where you belong, but you're probably the richest first baseman ever. And don't tell me some corn about you'd rather have the glory."

"Maybe it wouldn't be corn."

When he turned into 62nd Street the block was full of cars and he said, "Just as well I can't park. This street is so ritzy they'd arrest my old car for vagrancy. I'll let you off at the corner."

I laughed, but I was laughing at the Balton Towers. I was paying $350 a month for three rooms and a terrace and I was never in the place more than three or four months of the year. It was the only luxury I gave myself. But after the farm shack I was born in, the lousy 'home' that was more like a jail, and all the dusty hotel rooms I'd been in and out of, I got a bang living in one of the swankest apartment houses in town. My bathroom was bigger than our farm shack—and a damn sight better furnished.

As I thanked Alva and got out with my bag, he said, "Tomorrow at ten. When are you due back in Vero Beach?"

"I'm due in San Juan in two weeks."

"Then we'll have plenty of nights to talk baseball over a good supper."

The doorman was new. He gave my sweat shirt and cap a fast going over, then smiled as he said, "You *must* be Mr. Dolsan," and reached for my bag.

"That's me. And I'm still big enough to carry my own bag."

"Yes sir, Mr. Dolsan," he said, opening the door.

The drip at the desk was dressed like a funeral parlor receptionist. He said, "Good evening, Mr. Dolsan," as though I'd just stepped out, and took a thick pile of neatly tied letters from under the desk. "Here's your mail and messages, sir."

"All the boys get my Christmas cards?"

"Indeed we did, Mr. Dolsan. On behalf of the entire staff, thank you very much. Can I give you a hand with your bag?"

"Keep an eye on it. I'll be right back."

I went over to Lexington Avenue, walking fast to keep warm, found a delicatessen still open, I bought two bags of food and then went back, picked up my suitcase and the mail.

Unlocking my door, I snapped on the lights. The place looked fine—to me. My furniture is mostly heavy stuff, all solid and comfortable. I always admired stuffed leather chairs when I was coming up. Tossing my ball cap on one chair, my sweat shirt on another, I kicked my shoes off and padded along the thick carpets into the kitchen, put the groceries away. I lit a cigar and walked into the bedroom, dropping my clothes like a slob. I stretched out on my oversized Hollywood bed and blew a cloud of smoke at the ceiling. After living out of suitcases for almost a year, at last I was *home.*

After awhile I got hungry and did what I'd been looking forward to for months—went into the kitchen and made myself any damn thing I felt like. It turned out to be a large bowl of corn flakes and nuts, swimming in milk and chocolate syrup. You can't order *that* in a restaurant. I finished it and was considering a small steak, when the door bell rang. I was only wearing shorts, so I asked through the door, "Yeah?"

"Red, you miserable old bastard, it's me—Matt!"

I opened the door and Matt Blair came bubbling in. Matt is about my age but looks older, and lived across the hall.

He's a big time account executive, one of these jokers who never grew out of being an eager-beaver. He's also a baseball buff.

His silver-grey hair was carefully combed and brushed and he was dressed in a neat grey pin-stripe suit, a darker grey shirt, and a tie that might be called pale silver. We shook hands hard. He slapped my gut and told me I was in great shape and tan as a dirty behind, then went through the Dodger team, firing questions about everybody.

Matt was okay if you didn't get too big a dose of him. I didn't mind his questions, he never gave you a chance to answer them anyway.

Suddenly he glanced at his watch, shouted, "Red, get dressed. There is a goddamn soap-opera we have in the works and they're showing the pilot film tonight. Only take a half hour, then we'll stop in a new French restaurant I've discovered up on First Avenue and …"

"No dice, Matt, I've had restaurants and stool joints up to my …"

He burst out laughing, deep laughter, like a practiced actor. "I doubt if anybody ever called this place a 'stool joint'. We'll make it another night, have a bull session. But I really have something for you. New string of call girls and I've ordered one for myself. I'll buy you a girl for the night."

I suppose my face must have said something for he shook his head as he asked, "Is your puritan streak showing, or has one of those hot Porto Rican numbers staked you out?"

"Matter of fact, it's been a long time between gals for me, but I just got in and have lots of …"

Matt punched me on the shoulder. "You always were a loner, Red." He said 'loner' like he loved the word. "But I insist, these girls are wonderful. Tell you what, no party or anything like that, I'll send a girl up here. On me. Come to think of it I never sent you a Christmas present—this is it. Now, now, you can't refuse a gift. See you in the morning."

I was a little tense about seeing Doris' mother tomorrow, a girl might relax me. I felt restless and spent some time checking my fishing gear, oiling my shotguns. Then I turned on the bathroom radio to some good jazz, started a new cigar, took my mail and soaked in the tub. Matt was right, I was a loner: In over a year my mail didn't amount to more than a few dozen letters, most of them ads. That was why I never bothered having it forwarded.

There were a few Christmas cards, most of them from people I couldn't remember knowing, and one letter that looked like a *letter*. I threw away the ads and opened this letter.

June 10th.

Dear Lester:

I almost started off with Dear *Mr.* Dolsan. Isn't that funny? (Did I ever get to call you by your first name?) I have just learned from Mr. Blair that you are out of the country. If you ever received my phone messages, please disregard them. I was a little hysterical last month but I'm okay now. (God how I hate that word! So short and hard, like a bark. Okay! Okay!) I was in some difficulty which I realize now doesn't really concern you. So that is that.

Always remember me,

Peggy

I leafed through the phone messages: There were lots of them. Mostly, "Say Jack called," or "Pete from Baltimore," or Harry, Joe, Dick—names that didn't mean a thing to me. A baseball scout has to be on good terms with strangers, never knowing where a good tip will come from. There were three messages from Peggy Fulton, all dated a week or two before her letter.

The first message read: "A Miss Peggy Fulton wants you to call her," and had a phone number. The second message was on the following day. "Please call me. Very important. Please." The third message was four days later and simply said, "Miss Fulton called."

I read the letter again. The handwriting was short and jerky, almost childish, the Peggy Fulton signed with a flourish. It wasn't her right name anyway, not that it mattered. "Always remember me." I had thought about her down in Porto Rico, the way she cried in my arms. She had either been one of the very real or very phony moments in my phony life. I stared at the date on her letter—that was about eight or nine months ago.

Matt Blair is always giving sudden parties and most times I turn them down. Matt means well but he likes showing me off as a kind of freak, which I suppose I am among his crowd of high powered advertising people, guys and dolls in radio, TV, and show business. The parties were usually short affairs; everybody getting bagged as fast as possible, straining to sound clever and gay repeating the latest gags and gossip. There was always somebody beating out good piano, sometimes there would be a one punch fight—even between the girls—or some jerk would slap his gal around. And of course there were always a couple of pigs who got sick.

It had been a lousy evening, raw and damp, and I'd been restless all week waiting to hear from the Dodger front office as to whether they were taking me on as a full time scout. So when Matt had asked me to join the "gang" across the hall, I went. The shindig was already a half hour old and everybody was high.

I worked on a beer and watched these odd people, all of them dressed the same, even talking the same. All bright boys and girls living in a refined atmosphere of hot air, a hollow little confident world all their own.

I was standing in a corner, trying to figure them out, when this girl—she didn't look over 22—came staggering over, looked me in the eye and said, "A beer drinker—by Christ, a peasant!"

She was slim, almost skinny, and not very pretty. She had a big featured face, like a lot of farm gals I've known, and her clothes didn't quite look like the others; they were cheaper. But she was just as phony, sporting a clipped British accent. Being an expert on such matters I know she was about ten minutes from passing out. I gave her a polite grin and she put her highball glass down, by dropping it on the rug, grabbed my shoulder to steady herself. For a second I thought she was going to get sick all over me. Then she said in a little voice, "Would you mind taking me out of here? I'd really appreciate it. I'm fed up."

"When did you decide all that?" I asked wondering what my fatal attraction was for female rumdums.

"I imagine I decided it about four months ago but I'm getting around to saying it for the first time now." She talked in that careful way some drunks talk—and walk—sort of holding herself in. "It's all *merde*. Do you know what means, beer drinker?"

I said I did.

She stared at me for another moment, her eyes dazed, then she sort of fell against me, whispered, "Please take me out of here. I feel very bad. I ask you because you look ... honest. I mean honest—real. Obviously not one of this breed, the *merde* breed."

"Honey all you need is some air and you'll ..."

"Then please, give me some air, quickly."

I didn't want her to get sick so we crossed the room, pushing jokers out of the way as I herded her toward the door. As we passed Matt's bedroom she said, "My coat and hat. I must get them. I went without too many meals to buy that stupid, wonderful coat."

I helped her pull a worn fur jacket from the pile on the bed but couldn't find her hat. She was swaying, so I pushed her across the hall and out onto my terrace. For a long time she held on to the rail, her eyes closed, then she said—still with the clipped accent, "Oh I feel much better. The air is so cold and wet. I try but I just can't take that rot gut."

"Why do you take it?"

"Because I have to, it's all part of the rat race. What an expression, rat race. A quick drink, a sharp dig, a fast dirty joke, a fast feel—everything sharp and fast. It all adds up to ... nothing very much, at least for me. Oh Lord, you're an ugly man, so ugly and bald you're beautiful. I'm Peggy Fulton."

"Les Dolsan."

"You look solid, sturdy. What the French call ... I don't recall what the French ..."

"You already told me, *merde*. Want some coffee?"

"Yes, thank you, after I get more of this wonderful air I will have some coffee with real cream, if possible." She took a deep breath, showing off her small breasts. "Yes, coffee."

As we walked into the kitchen she looked around, asked, "You work here?"

"I live here, this is my place."

"Really. Do you live alone?"

I nodded.

"I see."

"What do you see, Miss Fulton?" I asked brightly.

She leaned against the kitchen doorway. "*Miss* Fulton. Oh you are something *Mr.* Dolsan. And something very refreshing. Only please don't spoil things by feeding me dirty jokes or making passes. You see, I will sleep with you, but no jokes, fast lines, lies, seduction arguments, or the rest of the filth. I just want it to be clean as possible, merely invite me to spend the night with you."

She was looking away from me as she said this, her face flushed like a child showing off. "That's quite a line you're slipping me," I said, wondering if she was setting me up for some sort of badger game: I'd been taken by dames a couple of times although never for much. "But all that outspoken baloney belongs next door in Blair's zoo."

"No, please. Please! It isn't baloney," she said in a low voice, her whole body shaking as if she was either cold or frightened. "It's loneliness. I would never be able to say this next door. I hardly know why I'm saying it here, unless I'm still drunk. But somehow the moment I saw you I knew I was ... going to say it." She looked up at me, waiting. "Please, please, don't insult me by turning me down. I couldn't stand that. This once and I'll never bother you again. Oh please—I never thought it would be a bother. I know I am not beautiful but I am young and ..." She began to cry, hysterical tears.

I shook her. "What the hell is all this?"

She fell inside my arms, against me, her tears wetting my shirt. "Don't shake me," she mumbled.

"What's the pitch, what are you pulling?"

"Pulling?" She tried to push me away, then fell against me again. "I am very sorry but I can't take it anymore. I thought you would understand." Her voice was under control, clipped.

"Understand what?" I asked wondering if she was nuts.

"That I am *not* Peggy Fulton. I have a Polish name you would not be able to pronounce. I came from London a year ago. I am a file clerk in an advertising agency. And all of us are so bright and eager—and shallow. I have learned the *correct* words, scrimped to buy the *right* clothes, have a *good* address. I have done all that and I am still an outsider. That is why I cannot take it any longer. It took me months of work to be invited to parties like Mr. Blair's—I don't know what I expected them to be, but I hate them. And I'm still lonely. Two nights ago I was at a cocktail party where they had lovely big colored birds in a cage in the living room. Live birds! Lord, who are they to cage birds?"

"Birds? What's with you?"

"What I am trying to say, you are making it difficult to say. I am sick to death of being alone! I need love and I need it badly or I think I will go out of my mind. You see I mouth all the dirty jokes, the ones that go into details. I tell them with a smile like a bright sophisticated girl—how I hate that word: *sophisticated*—it means nothing. And all the time I feel more of an outsider because I know not—how you say—I am a bluff, taking about something I know nothing about. I know you think I am a tramp, another cruel American word, but I have never been with a man!"

"Look, Miss Fulton, if you're trying to pull one of the oldest …"

"Here, this is what I am 'pulling'!" She said, pushing me away and ripping her left sleeve. There was a number tattooed in blue on her left arm. She said loudly, "They would ostracize me but really they would be afraid of me. I would be haunting them. I could have it removed but I will never sink that low."

"What's the number mean?"

She stared at me for a long second, her eyes big with amazement, then she began to laugh, real crazy hysterical laughter. I shook her again. "What is it?"

"It's a concentration camp number, I was in a camp from the time I was 9 till I was fourteen. I saw my mother march to a gas chamber." She waved her arm in my face. "It is not a medal, or a matter of being proud, but only that I must never be ashamed of it! Here, in America, I thought I would find an end to my loneliness, but all I found was clever talk, the terrible cruel smart talk!"

She sort of collapsed against me again and started sobbing. I stroked her hair and when she raised her face I kissed her as hard as I could. After a moment I felt her lips moving against my cheek as she said, "Now you are sorry for me."

"Maybe I am. Does it make any difference?"

"No! I want nothing to matter except your arms around me powerful and secure. Hold me tightly as you can, hurt me. Ah, this is what I need, if only for a few minutes. Tighter, let me feel your strength ... darling."

Sitting in the tub, puffing on my cigar, I folded the letter and tossed it on the floor with the ads. Odd thing was, whenever I had thought of her, what I remembered was her saying, *"Lord, who are they to cage birds?"*

Peggy Fulton, from a concentration camp to the Madison Avenue hustle. I looked at the dates on the phone messages. The poor kid probably thought she was caught when she'd tried to call me. But in the letter she said she was okay, so she must have come around. Or did she somehow hear I had dough and was trying for a big bite? That's about the only trouble with having folding money; it makes you suspicious of everybody.

I put on a robe. While I had the closet opened I checked on my winter suits and overcoats—I probably hadn't worn them a dozen times since I bought 'em. Then I looked over my bookshelf, mostly a collection of history and travel books I like to read and reread. I stretched out on the couch and watched TV for a few minutes.

I felt good. I was home. I could do anything I wanted to—only I didn't know what I wanted to do.

I was in the kitchen, cutting lots of onions and peppers for the steak, when the phone rang. The desk clerk said too-politely, "A young lady to see you, sir."

I'd almost forgotten Blair and his girls. I was a trifle annoyed, I wanted to finish cooking. But I told him to send her up.

She was a tall slim girl with a pretty face and lovely brushed red hair. Perhaps a trace of hardness in her eyes or it could have been my imagination. She wore a simple cloth coat with a tiny fur collar. I said hello and she said, "Hi," and looked around the place quickly. I took her coat and she was wearing a plain dark dress with a white collar. She looked like a school girl—maybe she was. She smiled at me, waiting for me to say something, then walked over to the terrace doors, said. "My, you have a fine view."

I finally went over and stood beside her. "Guess it's not bad," I said. Real bright conversation.

She gave me a big grin, ran a hand over my almost bald noggin. "Nice tan, Florida?"

"Yeah. Flew in a few hours ago."

"I was thinking of going down there this season. But I didn't."

There was a moment of awkward silence, then she slowly walked around the living room, went into the bedroom. I went back to the kitchen, put the food away. When I stepped into the bedroom she was sitting on the bed in the nude, glancing at an old hunting magazine I had.

She stripped big.

Later I got my robe on and asked if she wanted something to eat. She said, "No. Got a drink working?"

"No."

"All right if I get some sleep?"

"Sure."

In the kitchen I started preparing my steak and all of a sudden I put it back in the refrigerator. I'd really been looking forward to coming home and at that moment I knew I'd been kidding myself. This wasn't home—only a bigger hotel room. I could putter around in the kitchen—a big deal. It wasn't anything and there was even a stranger in my bed. Hell, I didn't even know her name.

I awoke her up and she gave me a big mechanical smile that faded as I said, "Honey, you mind taking a walk, going home?"

"Aren't you happy with me?"

"You're a doll. It's … told you I just came in. I remembered I have to go some place."

"Anything you say." She dressed quickly and I took three tens out of my wallet.

She looked at the money, hesitated a minute, then said, "That's okay, I've already been taken care of."

"I know it. This is something extra for spoiling your sleep."

"Well, say, thanks, mister."

At the door she gave me a card with her phone number. I tore up the card, threw a clean sheet and a blanket on the couch and went to sleep. One thing I could always do right—pound my ear.

CHAPTER TWO

I AWOKE AT SEVEN, still feeling restless. I stepped out on the terrace to get some air. It was the start of another clear but cold day. If it was this cold down at Vero Beach, it would play hell with stiff muscles. There was about 20 feet between my terrace and Matt's. He was wearing a sweater over his bathrobe and doing setting up exercises. He looked comical.

When he saw me he started taking deep breaths and slapping his fat chest. "This is what I need more of, Red, I'm too soft. How was last night?"

"Wonderful," I said because that was what he wanted to hear.

He leaned against the railing. "Tell you, Red, it's the only sensible way of living. And I speak as a five times married man, although three marriages were to the same woman. My dear screwy Flo. World is too full of complexes today. Can't have a relationship with a woman without taking on her troubles. I have my own: I don't ask anybody to share mine and I don't want to become involved in theirs. But then I don't have to tell *you*, Red."

I knew that last remark was coming. I didn't like the idea of shouting at each other, but fifteen stories up is a form of privacy, I said, "Matt, you remember last year, about a month before I went to Porto Rico—that would make it about the end of March—I met a girl named Peggy Fulton at a party you gave. I've been thinking about her. Do you know where she is?"

"Now Red, I give a lot of parties. Peggy Fulton? Never heard of her. She a singer or a ...?"

"Just a file clerk. You remember, we awoke you the next morning to find her hat. You were hungover and sore as hell."

Matt began waving his arms around, shaking his heavy shoulders—like an idiot athlete. "Oh yes, I recall that, a very plain babe. Flo was staying over and she didn't want the girl to see her, so …"

"Okay Matt, spare me your romances. What about Peggy Fulton?"

He leaned on the rail again, puffing a bit. "Let me think. I'm pretty sure we don't have any Peggy Fulton working for us. Flo was at the party because … yes, yes, all comes back to me: We were splitting a TV show with another sponsor and Flo's agency had the account, so I suppose this girl worked in Flo's office. That would be why Flo wouldn't want to be seen in my place in the morning. I'll call Flo and ask her. Peggy Fulton—something special about her?"

"No. I … eh … found a Christmas card from her. That's all. She said you told her I was out of the country."

"Me? Maybe she means Flo told her. Going to be home? I'll phone you about ten-thirty."

"I have to be at my lawyer's. I'll call you at your office sometime during the day."

"I'll leave a message if …" Matt began as a girl's voice called him from within his apartment.

He waved at me, walked off the terrace grinning like a fool.

I put the coffee on, took a bath and a careful shave, got out my best tweed suit, and wondered why I was dressing for my witchy mother-in-law. The phone range. It was a Porto Rican named Carlos Orta who had been a lot of things, including a lousy lightweight pug. He said in Spanish, "Excuse the early call, Les, but I am on my way to work. I came to see you, my friend, but you have a funny doorman. He does not like the color of my skin. I do not wish to start an argument, it would do neither of us any good. But this is a very bad thing."

"When was this?"

"A few minutes ago."

"Carlos, where are you now?"

"A drugstore over on 3rd Avenue. Do you wish to meet me here?"

"Carlos, I wish you to have breakfast with me in my apartment. I insist upon it, as a personal favor. Come right up." When he hung up, I called the desk and asked who was on the door. It was another new man. The clerk put him on the phone. I told him, "This is Lester Dolsan. A friend of mine claims you just treated him badly. Now wait, I know his face is brown and his nose is busted, and his clothes are probably worn. But he *asked* for me. I pay rent in this high class rat trap. It isn't up to you to decide who I'm going to see and who I'm not going to see. Don't you ever turn away *anybody—anybody—*who asks for me."

"I didn't know, Mr. Dolsan. His clothes were …"

"It isn't up to you to judge my friends' clothes. Look, you know now, so if this ever happens again—I'll fix your wagon."

"It won't happen again, sir," he said, the words crawling. "I'm new here, sir. I hope you'll overlook this, sir, not complain to the manager."

"Hell, I'm no fink. I never intended to complain to anybody. When I said I'd fix your wagon I meant I'll come down and beat your ears back. And don't think I can't! Now let's forget it."

By the time I got the living room straightened there was a knock at the door and Carlos Orta stood there. He was wearing a busted cap, worn dungarees, and a dirty windbreaker. His battered face broke into a big smile as he shook my hand, said, "Hey, this time he almost carry me to the elevator."

The doorman could: Carlos never weighed over 130 pounds in his life.

We talked in Spanish. I told him how sorry I was and Carlos said the hell with it and we bulled about San Juan as I dressed. I cooked ham and eggs and strong coffee while Carlos told me he was pushing a freight truck in the garment district. "Perhaps I make big mistake living up here. True, one makes good wages but the rest of it is bad, everything is cold: the weather, the houses, the people. However I didn't come to tell you my troubles. I have a cousin who lives in Lajas. This is a small village near San German. He has a boy, a stepson of 14, named Mike. My cousin writes this Mike is a remarkable pitcher. He also hits a ball well. You understand, he is but a boy. However in school games he has pitched three shutouts. This is not a matter of family pride. I have written to others in the village and they too say the boy throws a ball so fast it cannot be seen. I thought my friend, Les, would be interested."

"I am very much interested. Has this Mike played in San German or any large towns yet?"

"No. No other baseball man even knows of him. Yesterday I called the Dodger office for your best address, they tell me I can find you here. I am surprised and happy to learn you are in New York. But I never come this house again. Les, why you live in such a place?"

"I was asking myself that last night. Carlos, be certain the unpleasantness shall not happen again."

"I know, but I still will not come here."

"Where can I find you?"

He wrote down an address in East Harlem, added, "There is no names in the bells and the bells themselves are things of the past. It is a very poor house. Just go to the second floor and to the back. They all know me."

"Write your cousin—I will most certainly come to see him in June, at the very latest."

"I have already told him you will come and the boy is not to sign with anybody but you. I said you would see he gets the fair deal, if he is good. Here is the name and address in Lajas. They all know my cousin down there, he was a soccer player in his youth. Now I must leave, I have lost time from work."

"I will try to see you again but I may be very busy. A personal problem has brought me back here," I said, walking him to the door.

"If we do not meet here, this summer I expect to return to San Juan to see my family. We go fishing together there, as always. I am glad to see you looking so healthy, my friend."

We bulled about players and the latest crop of San Juan pugs for a moment. His shoes were cracked and old. I took out my wallet, told him, "You understand, baseball is my business. You have helped me in a business way. Purely as a business deal, kindly accept a hundred dollars." I only had a few tens. I took out a check and a pen.

"That is not necessary."

"I am not giving it to you. The club will repay me," I lied. "Remember, if he gets the breaks, this Mike can make thousands of dollars for the Dodgers. The Dodgers give this money to you as a small token of their thanks."

"From you I would not take it, from the Dodgers—yes. Some friends of mine are in trouble, need money."

I wrote a check, made it out to CASH, gave it to him. When he left I put the kid's name and address down in my notebook, slipped on my overcoat. It was a few minutes after nine.

After stopping at the desk to cash another check, I took a cab to Hanns' office. I was as jumpy as a bag of cats.

Alva said, "Glad you're early, Red. We have a few things to go over. First: let me do the talking. And try to keep your temper—that's most important. We both know the old lady is a psycho, undoubtedly she'll rave and rant at you. But keep in mind we want her to sign this settlement—that's what you came up North for. We have to grin and take her ravings—otherwise I'd tell her to go to blazes, have the case thrown out of court when she contests the will. If you start arguing with her, she won't sign. So you take it and keep still. Understand?"

"Yeah. After we sign, then what?"

"The court has to approve, of course, and then the will is probated. I can rush that along. Invested conservatively, and Mrs. Andrews' attorney and I have agreed on the various government bonds in which we shall invest the principal, your yearly income will be about $14,000."

"Who cares? I have money. And there'll always be a way for me to earn my living in baseball—I hope. Probably all of the fourteen grand will go down the tax drain anyway."

Hanns smiled. "Maybe you should marry a widow with a dozen kids. Seriously, Red, I keep telling you to consult a CPA. There's ways of lessening the tax bite. Run a large farm—at a loss—and in ten years you'll end up with a well developed piece of land worth double what you put into it, with taxes paying it all. Or back a small business that looks sad and ..."

His secretary phoned in that the witch had arrived with her lawyer. I felt my nerves jump, sweat starting down my sides. Actually the whole damn business took under a half hour but it seemed like a long year to me. I was trying to click with a Canadian team when Doris died and I buried her in Toronto, knowing full well it would be too much of a trip for the old lady—and also knowing the last person Doris would want at her funeral, or around her at any time, would be her mother. That meant I hadn't seen the old lady since the war, and she'd looked like a monster then. Now she seemed fatter and more hunched over, like a large spider dressed in an old seal coat, a hat and veil hiding her wrinkled ugly face. A few ragged strands of mouse-grey hair hung from under the hat.

If everything about her was old and warped, her voice was still powerful and young. She didn't lose a second in slugging me with it. As she sat down she announced it was the first time she'd ever dirtied herself by sitting in the same room with a murderer. Her lawyer was embarrassed, tried to hold her to the business at hand. He knew damn well I was letting them take a half a million from me.

But the old witch hadn't even warmed up. She accused me of being a fortune hunter, said every cent Doris had really should be hers since it had all been made by her "late beloved husband." Alva tried to quiet her by reminding the witch I had an absolute legal right to the money. The old lady roared Doris was incompetent when she made out the will, incompetent when she married me, and all she wanted was a chance in court to prove what an alcoholic I'd made of "my sweet innocent daughter, my dearest Doris." Then she started on her favorite tune: how I'd 'driven' Doris to suicide, and on and on.

Doris' drinking was a sensitive spot with me and I held myself in by silently thinking of the many things I could really tell the witch … the things Doris had confessed to me in her various drunken moments of truth.

I wanted to ask why she drove Doris nuts as a kid with her desire to be 'society' after old man Andrews started making big money when Doris was about 13? They gave her the works, even a Swiss finishing school and the nearest thing they could get to a coming-out party. And Doris miserable and ashamed, having to face and endure the cold shoulder and constant snub 'society' handed her. Or why the old bitch forced Doris into a fast marriage with a rummy nance? It was strictly a cash and carry deal, his family was in the same business and the marriage saved the Andrews company. It was around then, when Doris was 19, that she really learned where the dough came from. Despite the fancy letterheads and her father's swank office, every cent came from turpentine camps run mostly by convict labor. Doris even had to learn that the hard way—a con died from a whipping and there was a big stink in the papers. Doris left her prancing husband and took up with a bottle.

Maybe the old man had conscience trouble too, the docs claimed he worried himself into cancer. Mrs. Andrews treated her daughter's drinking in her usual selfish manner: the old bag shut herself up in their country house while Doris was drinking her way across the country, pretended nothing was happening. Doris had another quickie marriage with some joker who was also hunting for himself in a cocktail glass, and an even faster divorce. A year later she married me.

Oh I could have told the old lady how Doris cursed her whether she was boiled or sober—and meant every horrible word. Or how the psychiatrist explained the old bitch's tender and idiotic love for animals. Believe me, I could have talked all over my mouth. And it all would have been the truth.

I should have told her to go to hell but all I did was keep quiet, take it. Everything was finally signed and the old lady left the office after telling me about my being illegitimate, that my mother had been a whore, and all the rest of it. She had paid a private dick to dig this up when I first married Doris. I never believed the stuff about my mother, but then I never knew for sure.

The detective earned his dough the hard way. He spent several weeks in the hospital after I caught up with him.

Anyway, Mrs. Andrews crawled out of the office and Alva looked at me like a second staring at a punchy fighter, said, "Red, let's have lunch together? You need to be around somebody, talk this out and …"

"Nope, I'm okay. You don't get sore when you're in the zoo and a caged ape screams at you. No, not an ape, a hyena." As a matter of fact, I did feel beaten but also good—at least I'd kept Doris' name from being dragged through the mud … and kept myself in baseball. And I really didn't know, or care, which was the real reason.

I started for the door, said, "I'll be in touch, Alva."

"Red, are you certain you're all right? You look … well, sickly."

"Hell with that old bag. I'm fine."

"How about supper? After all, you know the way I love to chew the rag about baseball."

"Okay. I'll call you."

"No, no, let's make it definite. How's five thirty at Costello's on 3rd Avenue?"

"I'll be there," I said, shaking hands and walking out.

Twice I've been beaned by a ball, I mean a real hard beaning. The worst time I knew exactly what was happening as they carried me off the field and into an ambulance. Of course that was in the days when they never heard of head protectors. The other time, I suddenly came to in a movie theatre the same night and hadn't the faintest idea how I'd got there, although they told me I seemed okay when I walked out of the locker room.

It was something like that now. In a daze I got on the subway and found myself in downtown Brooklyn—perhaps I was heading for the Dodger office for some reason. Then suddenly I was in the steam room of the Hotel St. George and I seemed to have sweated all the hate out of me. I took a swim in the pool and got dressed.

It was twelve-twenty and I was hungry. I phoned Matt and asked if he wanted to have lunch and he said, "Sorry, Red, I'm at the start of a sales conference, having lunch in. Oh, by the way," he dropped his voice to a whisper, "I spoke to Flo about Miss Fulton. She vaguely remembered her. She left the office months ago. Quite a stir—she swallowed the watermelon."

"She did what?"

"Red, as an old farm boy you should know what I'm talking about—she was pregnant. Also unmarried. Flo remembers because it caused the usual office gossip about ... Red, *you?*"

"Cut the clowning, Matt, I told you I found a Christmas card and was ... eh ... merely asking. Flo know her address? I'd like to send the kid a gift or something."

"No, she doesn't. Flo said the office had gotten around to raise a few bucks for the girl, but she'd moved. They never could locate her ..."

Pregnant.

"... Red, I hope you're not in this."

"Are you crazy?" *Pregnant.* I said something about Matt having a suspicious mind and he told me an old joke. *Pregnant.* I hung up and lit a cigar.

Pregnant.

Damn, but the old ball was sure bouncing all over the place this morning.

CHAPTER THREE

S o that was the play—I had a kid.

I started walking because I can think best when I'm sitting still and at the moment I didn't want to think. I walked across Brooklyn Bridge getting my usual kicks out of seeing the Manhattan skyline. Long about the middle of the bridge I got my cigar going again, stopped to watch the boats on the river below me and out in the harbor—all of them work boats. A lot of buzzing in my noggin told me maybe I was taking too much for granted, being a sucker. The one time, the first time, girls don't get pregnant, except in books. For all I knew Peggy had been sleeping around since then. Yet I *knew* it was mine, I had a hunch, and I've been a hunch player all my life. I was *certain* it was mine. It added up right. Why else would she be calling me, writing me?

I knocked some ashes down at the river. There were only two things I could do about it: Do nothing or do everything.

If I wanted to forget it I could. That letter had been months ago, Peggy probably would never get in touch with me again. It wouldn't have taken much effort to get my San Juan address from Matt's wife.

If I did something about it, then she had me over a small barrel: I'd have to do exactly what Peggy wanted—I sure couldn't stand a court case or any stink. I didn't really know much about Peggy, yet I didn't see her as a chiseler. And there was the kid, *my* kid. The idea I had helped make a child was as astonishing to me as if I'd popped a fly ball at a flying saucer.

Okay, what could I do for my kid? What did I want to do? I wanted the kid raised right, that meant a regular home with a poppa around. Marrying Peggy was a crazy idea, still a kid was as good a reason, or maybe a better one, then most married people start with. Odd the way I'd found myself thinking of marriage lately. Guess a man can be alone only so much. There was the other side of the coin too: I was also the clown who knew the hell an unhappy marriage could be. Sometimes Doris talked of having a child. Maybe that was another reason for her drinking—some organ was wrong side up and she never could have a baby. She ...

I suddenly threw my cigar in the air and hooted out loud. What a set-up I had! Aside from doing 'right' by Peggy and the kid, I'd over-looked the real big deal—*I had a kid,* under the terms of the agreement I'd just signed that kid would come into a half a millon bucks! And best of all I could picture the old witch having a fit about it!

Hell, the half a million sure made a difference, Peggy might be so happy over the kid getting it she might not insist upon marriage. And I was silly worrying about a scandal—she could have raised a stink long ago. The main thing was—somewhere in the city Peggy Fulton and my kid were having tough sledding. The first thing was to find them. We could take our time, I'd take Peggy and the kid down to San Juan and we could talk it through. Then we'd see.

I walked over the bridge and took a cab up to the Balton Towers. In the lobby they had phone books for the four boroughs but I didn't see any Peggy Fulton. I went up to my place and phoned the first hospital I came across in the book, asked if they could tell me if a Peggy Fulton had given birth there during December or January.

This seemed to amuse the woman at the other end of the phone. She asked who I was and when I said a friend of Miss Fulton's, she told me, "I'm sure you must realize we can't give out information of this kind. Not even to members of the family. No hospital will. Sorry."

I phoned a sport writer I'd done a lot of fishing with. After we'd made the usual small talk and he told me how sore he was he didn't make the trip to Vero Beach this year, I said, "Bill, I need a favor."

He laughed. "Things can't be so tough *you're* putting the bite on people. You're playing first base on the Fort Knox team, I hear."

"Look, cut the corn for a second. There's a relative of mine, a young fellow who thinks he ... well, got a girl knocked-up. We've tried the hospitals but they won't give us the right time. Can you, as a newsman, find out if a Peggy Fulton gave birth during last December or January in any New York City hospital?"

"I've done a lot of screwy favors, Red, but this tops them. Think I can find that out. Get somebody to check at the Board of Health. Mrs. or Miss?"

"Miss."

"Oh. Sure of the name and that she had the kid here in the city?"

"I know the name," I said, thinking I really didn't—she might have had the kid under her real name, whatever that was. "As for having it here, we think so."

"I'll try. Call me back about five. Red, interested in surf-casting for flounders and small bass out on Long Island?"

"No time, Bill. I'm here on business and have to get back to the island soon."

"Okay. Call between four and five—relative."

I made myself coffee and a hell of a western sandwich, was surprised at how good I felt. Mrs. Andrews would snap her ancient stack all right. I dug up the phone messages Peggy had left, dialed the number she'd given on one of them. A deep-voiced woman answered. When I asked for Peggy Fulton there was a moment of silence followed by, "Why Peggy hasn't lived here since … oh … last October."

"Any idea where she moved to?"

"She didn't leave any forwarding address."

"May I ask who you are? Any relation of Miss Fulton's?"

"Sure you may ask, I was her landlady. Why do you want to see her …? Say, are you … *him?*"

The word popped out of the receiver and I could picture her fish-mouth working. "No. I know about her … eh … condition. But for certain other reasons, I'm interested in locating Miss Fulton. Look, would it be possible for me to speak to you in person? Now?"

"Yes. I don't see what harm it can do. Are you the F.B.I.?"

"No m'am. I'll explain when I see you."

She told me her name was a Mrs. Lubeck and gave me a West 4th Street address. I said I'd be right down.

Outside, I told the doorman to get me a cab. He was young and beefy. I slipped him a buck tip when he opened the cab door and he said, "Thank you, Mr. Dolsan."

"You outweigh me 50 pounds. But I can still take you," I said and he gave me the dopey stare of a guy who doesn't know if he's being kidded or not.

Sitting back in the taxi, I wondered what yarn I'd tell Mrs. Lubeck. I hadn't given her my name over the phone. Until I actually found Peggy it would be smart to use a phony name and story.

The house was one of these small walk-up apartments that would have become a tenement long ago if the Village wasn't so popular. Mrs. Lubeck didn't look like I'd pictured her over the phone at all. She was a small plump woman with grey hair in a bun, worn print dress, and a rather motherly face. I'd expected a business woman, a harder type. I asked, "Mrs. Lubeck? I'm Matt Hanns. I spoke to you over the phone."

"Oh yes. Do come in Mr. Hanns. Well, you are a surprise. I expected a younger man—you know what I mean."

I didn't know what she meant but followed her down a long hallway with rooms leading off it. She took me to a plain little living room with some violently colored paintings on the wall that didn't make any sense to me, but the colors were interesting. She sat down on a couch and crossed her fat legs, offered me a cigarette, then lit one herself when I turned it down. Blowing twin clouds of smoke through her nose, she asked in that deep voice that didn't go with her face, "Now Mr. Hanns, exactly what is your business with Miss Fulton?"

"I represent an insurance company, the California Mutual, and we have a small policy on which Miss Fulton is the sole beneficiary. I was in touch with her office and they gave me this phone number," I said, lying smoothly.

"Shame Peggy isn't here, she could use the money. I have no idea where she is. As I told the F.B.I. she left here in October and …"

"The F.B.I.?"

"She was an alien, a refugee. I knew that all along although she never talked about it. Seems all aliens are required to register every year, in January, I think. Anyway, she didn't register and they came around to ask about her. I imagine this was the last address she gave. I don't know why they didn't go to her office…. What was the name of the company she worked for?"

"Why, the … the … B-Blair Advertising Company," I stammered.

Mrs. Lubeck gave me a sharp look, then a grin cut her face. "Indeed it was not! You've been lying to me, Mr. Hanns, haven't you? You *are* the man who got her in trouble, aren't you?"

"I must have got the name of the company mixed up with another...."

"Mr. Hanns, stop lying. I really don't see the point of lying, it's done!"

I shrugged. "I'll level with you, Mrs. Lubeck: I knew Peggy for a very short time, one night to be exact. I've been out of town for almost a year. I returned yesterday and heard about her being pregnant. I'd like to find her."

"Just one night? Really?"

"Only a half a night, *really!*"

"Well. But I am glad to see a man your age showing some sense. Tell you, Mr. Hanns ... That is your true name?"

"Yes."

"You see I make my living renting out rooms in two apartments I have here. Lot of kids come to New York and want to live in the Village. Most of them think a Village address will give them a touch of genius. Of course the Village is a fraud these days. I remember it when Boden-heim was a young poet, O'Neill, Floyd Dell, and others were writing. Artists and poets really lived here. I've written some poetry myself, in my day."

"Was Peggy a writer?"

"No, no. None of them have any talent now. They just come here and try to be so very, very Bohemian. They wear old clothes and talk cleverly, never realizing art is a severe taskmaster. They actually are very average youngsters. Maybe they make love and all that, but in the end they marry and settle down like people in Parsnips Corners do. I had two other girls who were 'in trouble,' and they tried to act very casual about it, and all the time they would have died if their boyfriends hadn't married them.

However, with Peggy it was different. She was always a lonely little thing, kept to herself a great deal. And when the baby began to show, she was terrified. I took an interest in her, partly selfish, because when she lost her job ... I'm not running a home here, I didn't want her to run up a lot of rent."

"Sure. And you have no idea where she is now?" I said, trying to cut this short.

"No. I suggested she contact an organization that helps unwed mothers but I don't think she ever did. Perhaps being an alien she was afraid she'd be deported. She was working at odd jobs, sales girl, a day here or there, and about a month before she left here the poor thing seemed—more relaxed. She had some money. I know she paid me all she owed. One Sunday in October she suddenly told me she was moving and that was the last I saw of her. Wonder if she had a girl or a boy?"

"Did she have any relatives? Haven't you any idea where she could have gone?"

"No. She kept to her room a good deal those last weeks—she was getting big. Except for going to a doctor every ..."

"Recall the name of the doc?"

"No, I don't. But I do remember she got several phone calls. You know, being here most of the day ... well, I couldn't help but overhear some of her conversations. Really, I couldn't help it." Mrs. Lubeck let me have a fat smile. "I think she was talking to a lawyer, but I never did catch the name. And as I said, Peggy wasn't the confiding kind. Oh yes, I do remember a Mrs. Hemingway phoned once or twice. Left a Staten Island number. I remember because the name was the same as that of the writer and I meant to ask Peggy if they were any relation. Also, because I used to have a cousin in Staten Island. That's all I know."

All this left me standing still. "What was Mrs. Hemingway's first name?"

Mrs. Lubeck shrugged her plump shoulders.

"Has anybody in the neighborhood seen Peggy since then?"

"I doubt it. She wasn't the kind that hung around the bars or cafe espresso places. On account of my cousin, I happen to have a State Island phone book around some place. Perhaps you can look up Hemingway."

She left the room and returned a minute later with an old and stained phone book. There were two Hemingways listed in Staten Island: Joseph Hemingway and a Robert Hemingway. I wrote down the addresses and numbers, thanked her as I stood up.

At the door she asked, "Are you married?"

"Me? No. Why do you ask?"

"You know why: if you do find Peggy you'll be able to do the right thing. I wish you luck. Let me know what happens, Mr. Hanns. Of course I'm interested."

I'll bet you are! I thought as I said I would be sure to keep in touch with her.

"I think it's a nice thing you're doing. Poor Peggy, always the simple quiet ones that surprise you. She was really a nice kid."

"I know, she didn't like to see birds caged," I said, walking out. Mrs. Lubeck called out something but I kept going.

Downstairs I looked at the two numbers, decided it would be silly to call: nobody would discuss a thing like this over the phone. I hailed a cab, gave him the address of Joseph Hemingway. The cabbie was a hard looking joker and as I opened the door he said, "Wait up, Mac. Staten Island is a long haul. I may not get a return fare."

"Okay, don't let it upset your day. I'll either come back with you or make it worth your while."

It was an interesting ride. New York City is so big some parts always look new. The ferry ride was a kick and Staten Island itself seemed a thousand miles away from Times Square. I sat back, relaxed, sneaking in a smoke on the ferry. One thing, I had to lie better—Mrs. Lubeck spotted me as poppa from the go.

Joseph Hemingway lived in a large neat brick house not far from the ocean, or maybe it was a bay. I told the cabbie to wait and rang the bell. A tall thin woman with a lantern jaw and fuzzy blonde hair opened the door. She was wearing a red house coat that matched her lipstick and her large square-shaped red earrings. I tipped my hat and asked, "Mrs. Joseph Hemingway?"

"Yes." She looked and talked like she was thinking of a lot of things—none of them about talking to me.

"I'm from the California Insurance Company and …"

"We have insurance."

"I'm not selling insurance. I'm looking for a young woman named Peggy Fulton. She was friendly with people named Hemingway out here. Do you know her?"

"No."

"It will be to her benefit if I can locate her. Did you ever hear the name Peggy Fulton?"

"No."

"Would your husband know her—perhaps she worked in his office?"

"No."

"Do you know any other Hemingways out here?"

"No."

She had me licked. She kept staring at me as though I was a picture window. Finally I said, "This is important, settling an estate. Maybe your husband could give me some information. When can I see him?"

She raised her head a bit as if getting ready to sing and called out, "Joey."

Joey turned out to be a guy with a thick neck and a real beer belly. He was decked out in a worn thick sport shirt, blue slacks, and slippers. Before I could ask him anything he said in a slightly shrill voice, "I overheard you talking to my wife. I never heard of any Miss … Whatever her name is, neither did the wife. She told you that."

"Merely checking on …"

"Stop annoying my wife," Joey said, closing the door.

"Annoying her? She's safe—all she can say is no," I said as the door slammed in my face.

Back in the cab I gave him the other address and the cabbie shook his head, told me, "I'll have to ask. Don't know where I am out here."

"Okay, ask."

He drove around till we reached a kind of shopping center and the cabbie asked a cop and soon we stopped in front of an old wooden two family house. There were two bells and two names— none of them Hemingway. I rang the bottom bell. A young kid of about 16 in a sweat shirt and dungarees opened the door, said, "Whatever you're selling, we don't need any, mister."

"A Robert Hemingway live here?"

He shook his head. "Used to, but they moved a couple of months ago."

"Where did they move to?"

"I don't know, never left any address. You a cop?"

"No. I'm from an insurance company and looking for …"

"Insurance?—I heard something about Mrs. Hemingway being sick."

"Look, I'm interested in a friend of theirs, a Miss Peggy Fulton. You ever hear of her?"

"Nope. Like I said, they were away a lot. I mean, most of the day. Both worked in Manhattan. Kind that kept to themselves."

"Any idea how I can get in touch with Mr. Hemingway, know where he works?"

"No I don't. I think he was a salesman. Funny thing, I saw him a few days ago down in Washington Square. I go to NYU. Saw him as I was rushing to school. He always was a sharp dresser but this time he was really togged out. I called to him and he waved at me. I didn't have time to stop and talk."

"Anybody in the neighborhood who might know where they are? Any friends or relations?"

He shook his head. "Told you, they kept to themselves."

"How about your folks, would they know where I could find them?"

"Nope. Mom was remarking how odd it was we never get a card or anything from them. Moved sudden, too. But I heard some place that Mrs. Hemingway was pretty sick, or something. She was a nice woman."

"They didn't leave any forwarding address for their mail?"

"Mister, I told you they didn't. Guess they put in a change of address in the Post Office, we don't get any mail for them."

"Where's the Post Office?"

"See that traffic light down there? Make a right and it's about five blocks."

"Well, thanks. When did you say they moved?"

"Let's see. It was before Christmas. Maybe in November."

I thanked him and went back to the cab.

At the Post Office I told a man at the Inquiry window what I wanted and he said, "We can't give out forwarding addresses. Not allowed."

"But this is something to their advantage. An insurance policy they can collect on," I said, wondering what I'd do if he asked to see my credentials."

"You can write them and we'll forward it, if they put in a change of address. Wait a minute, I'll look. Did you try the phone? Phone company might have a new number for them."

"I'll do that," I said, feeling like a fool.

"I'll look them up the carrier's beat book, meantime."

There was a booth in the lobby and I dialed the number Mrs. Lubeck had found in her phone book. After a few rings the operator told me, "Sorry, the number has been disconnected, the party has moved."

"Have they a new number?"

"No sir, there isn't any listed for them."

I hung up and went back to the Inquiry window. The man there said, "We have a change of address for them. You write them at the old address and it will be forwarded."

"Look, why can't you tell me where they are? You just saw the new address. Hell, it will take a couple of days for them to get my letter and I have to see them in a hurry."

"You write them now, send it Special Delivery. It's almost three—they should have your letter by tonight. That's the best I can do for you."

"Sure there's not a quicker way than that?" I asked, staring at him as I took out my wallet.

He said quietly, "You don't want to do that, mister," and walked away from his window.

I started toward the Stamp window, then turned around and walked out to the cab and told him to take me back to Manhattan. If I sent a card and told them to call me, I'd have to give my real name and phone number. I wasn't sure I wanted to do that.

When we stopped for a light I got a better idea and told the cabbie to drive back to the Post Office. He glanced at the meter. We were over nineteen bucks and he looked worried.

38

At the Post Office I bought a card and a Special stamp, addressed the card to Mr. Robert Hemingway at his old address. On the back I wrote:

Dear Mr. Hemingway:

If you know the whereabouts of a Miss Peggy Fulton, would appreciate your calling me late this evening at IThaca 5-6791. Be to her advantage. Looking for her to settle an estate. If you have any information, would appreciate hearing from you.

Frank Ross

I handed this to the guy at the Inquiry window and went back to the cab feeling like a super detective. That wasn't my phone exchange, but since there are three letters in every opening on the dial, when they dialed I T, they would be also dialing my exchange, and the rest of the number was my phone.

I had the cabbie take me to downtown Brooklyn. I got off at Montague Street and the meter read $23.65. I gave him three tens and told him to keep the change.

The cabbie gave me a big, "Thanks a million, Mac. Had you pegged all wrong, thought you were a dead one."

"I'll wear my tux the next time I ride with you."

I dropped into the Dodger office and bulled with the boys. Although the islands were my specialty, I also scouted semi-pro teams from Florida to New Orleans. It means a lot of jumping about and I didn't like the idea, but that was the job. A busy part-time ivory hunter had sent in tips on a hot ball hawk in the backwoods of Georgia and a promising catcher playing high school ball in South Carolina. I got all the dope and records he'd sent in, was told how high I could go in signing them, and if necessary how much to piece off their parents, since they were both under age.

I phoned Bill when I left there and he said, "You can breathe easier, I checked the Board of Health—no record of any Peggy Fulton giving birth. I figured she might have given your 'relative's' name, so I checked for a Peggy Dolsan or a Mrs. Lester Dolsan—nothing. I trust you're properly relieved and ready to buy me a drink."

"Yeah, the next time I see you. You're full of enough corn now. Thanks anyway, Bill."

I was ten minutes late when I reached Costello's and Alva was sipping a beer in one of the booths and eating his way through a bowl of popcorn like a kid.

I sat down and he said he had a couple of steaks working and I said, "Alva, the old lady is in for a surprise—I have a kid!"

"You must have put in a very busy afternoon. What's the gag?"

"No gag," I said and told him all about Peggy, right from the time I took her out of Blair's party. I talked right through most of his steak and when I finished, finally started eating, he said, "This sounds fantastic, a one night stand and ..."

"I know, that seems a big joke to everybody. Maybe it's tough to believe but there it is: one night and one baby—that I can't find."

"Red, I'd do a lot of thinking about this before I made any moves. I realize how much you want to turn the tables on old Mrs. A, but ..."

"Sure I want to give the old bitch a legal licking, but it's more than that. I *have* been doing a lot of thinking. I'm not making any empty noble gesture. This is *my* kid and I'll be damned if I want him, or her, dragged up like I was. And there's Peggy—what she's been through, the years in a concentration camp. Is her pay-off to be busting her back in a shabby room, raising an unwanted kid? Sure, the half million will change everything for her and the kid, let me whack Mrs. Andrews where she's most sensitive, in her bankbook. But Alva, even if there wasn't that, I'd still find Peggy and the kid—I'm not exactly a poor slob and what the hell, all this is my responsibility, or at least part mine. I don't use my dough, let it do the boy and Peggy some good."

Alva lit a cigarette. "Your steak is cold but keep eating for a while and let me talk for a change. This has a lot of angles that must be considered before you take any steps. In the first place, you ought to decide *why* you're doing this—really for the kid's sake, or to get at Mrs. Andrews. It's important to know that and …"

"Why is that important? Kid gets helped no matter what."

"I'm going to explain why, if you give me a chance. Let's start off with the fact that you're looking for this Miss Fulton— she's not searching for you. How do you know there is a child? Her letter might mean she had an abortion, or more likely a miscarriage. The last anybody saw of her she was five or six months gone, they don't always make it, especially when under a strain. Then again, let us suppose she's had the baby, have you considered she might be married since then? Or she could have been married or engaged all the time—despite what she told you? Keep in mind that the reason she hasn't tried to contact you since the letter could be she isn't anxious to see you or have you find her."

"She can tell me all that when I find her—don't forget the salting money the kid will come into."

"That's exactly why I said to be certain in your own mind why you're doing this, Red. From what you say, this girl is young enough to be your daughter, to repeat a trite phrase, and you know very little if anything about her. You see, Red, under the law, the father of an out-of-wed-lock child has absolutely no rights to the child."

"What's that mean?"

"It means you can't even claim the child is legally yours, until you adopt the baby. To adopt the child you'd probably have to marry Miss Fulton."

"As an adopted child, would the boy come into the money?"

"Yes. Lord, are you seriously thinking of marrying the young lady?"

"I don't know. Off hand I'd say no. Still, to get the kid the money, what would be wrong if I did marry her, adopt the child, and I divorce Peggy a year later? Would that still be legal, far as the kid's money is concerned?"

"Once you've legally adopted the child, he's your heir. Divorce wouldn't change that. Red, you talk about marriage like it was having a cup of coffee. This young lady can be a fraud a ..."

"Alva, you heard the old bitch this morning, I was raised as a bastard. Okay, if I can do nothing more than change that for my kid, it's worth it. And I can do more—a half a million bucks more."

"You assume you can rid yourself of this young lady any time you wish—once she knows there's a half million involved, she'll never let go of you."

"The kid will have the money, not me. If she never lets go of him till he's 21, fine. Look, Alva, we're crossing bridges before we get to them. Let me find Peggy and the kid *first*, then I'll see what the set-up is."

"And if she's already married?"

I shrugged. "Where would that leave the kid in relation to the dough?"

"If she's married and has either put her husband down as the father, or if the husband has already adopted the child, you can't make the child your heir."

"Okay, even if she is married, I'd still like to do something for the boy—perhaps set up a trust fund for him with ten grand."

Alva grinned. "You keep saying boy, there's a lot of girls born every day. As for locating Miss Fulton, and I hope you really have thought out all the possible implications, remember she might have had the child any place in the country, not just in New York City. She could have relatives anywhere and gone to …"

"I got the impression she didn't know anybody here."

"You said she's a refugee. She couldn't have entered the country unless somebody put up a bond. You see the point I'm making, Red, you don't even know her real name, or anything about her. If you go blundering around, you'll tell this story to the wrong person and end up paying blackmail, be thrown out of baseball. If you want to find Miss Fulton and the child, go about it the right way."

"What way is that?"

"Hire a good private detective."

"I never even thought of that. Do you know one, a good one?"

"I know of a man who's capable, fast, and can be trusted. Let me see if I can reach him," Alva said, getting up.

"Be sure he owns a big tight mouth," I said as Alva headed for the phone booth. I'd finished a second cup of coffee when he returned and gave me a slip of paper with the name T. D. Temple and an address on West 29th Street. "This is his home address, Red. He wasn't keen about having you come there tonight but I explained you only have a few weeks in town. I didn't tell him anything except that you couldn't afford any publicity on the case. As I said, you can trust him, but it's up to you to tell him everything, or as much as you want."

"Sure. Thanks, Alva, I'll go right down there," I said, thinking there wasn't any sense in telling the dick about the money angle, very few guys can be trusted when there's a half a million involved.

I called for the check as Alva said, "This is on me. And don't argue, all part of my fee." He paid the tab and at the door said, "I'll go with you, if you like, but I don't see any point in it."

"Neither do I. I'll keep in touch with you. And Thanks again."

The West 29th Street address turned out to be one of these small new apartment buildings, nearly every window sprouting an air conditioning unit. Temple had a compact one room apartment, everything very smart and modern. He was wearing a silk robe over slacks, a white shirt and stubby red bow tie, and the last thing he looked like was a detective. He was so small and slight a lazy bunt would have knocked him over. His black hair was thin and his pale face had pinched, tight features, including a hair line moustache.

I said, "I'm Les Dolsan."

"Yes, of course. Do come in," he said, his voice slow and soft. He pulled a paper handkerchief out of his pocket, blew his nose carefully. "Have to excuse my sniffles. I'm trying to fight off a cold."

He took my hat and coat and I sat in a reed chair that looked like a large ice cream cone and turned out to be comfortable. Temple sat on a red couch opposite me that probably opened into a bed and poked at his nose with paper handkerchiefs as I told him about Peggy Fulton. He seemed to be bored. I wasn't exactly impressed by T. D. Temple.

I talked for about fifteen minutes and when I was done, Temple sat there almost half asleep, still playing with his nose. He didn't talk for awhile and finally I asked, "Want me to go over anything, so you can make notes?"

"Nothing to make notes about, so far, Mr. Dolsan," he said quietly, staring at me. "Your friend over the phone said you were a cracker-jack first baseman. Notice you're left handed, that makes it easier for a man at first to get off a throw."

"Did the man on the phone also tell you I have to leave town in about eight days, that I'm in a hurry to get this over with?"

Temple nodded. "Talking off the top of my head. I think I shall either find your Miss Fulton within a day, or I may not find her at all. Evidently the F.B.I. can't—which may or may not mean anything. Now, I charge fifty dollars a day, plus expenses. I'd like a retainer of $100. If after a few days, the case looks hopeless, I'll tell you so and not waste your money."

I took out my wallet and he said, "I'd rather have a check—shows you hired me."

I got a check out of my wallet and found my pen, asked, "What does the T. D. stand for?"

"Just make it out to T. D. Temple. That will do fine," he said like I was a backward school boy.

I gave him the check and he dropped it on a desk in one corner of the room then came back and draped himself on the couch again. "If I locate Miss Fulton, that's the end of the line for me. You understand you can't make her marry you or give up the child. In a case like this, a father has no rights."

"Find her and I'll take it from there."

"One thing more, from now on let me do the work. Don't do anything on your own. For instance, sending that Special Delivery card today wasn't a smart move."

"I was only trying to find this Robert Hemingway."

"I'll locate him the first thing in the morning, unless they've moved out of the city. I'll have his new address a few minutes after nine."

"Fast as that?" I said, trying to sound sarcastic.

He gave me a tight smile. "I shall not give you a course in tracing a person, Mr. Dolsan, but it really is very simple, in most cases. Every Christmas I send a few bottles of good Scotch to friends who work for the various utility companies. A man in the gas and electric company can tell me in a minute where the Hemingways have moved. So can my friend in the phone company."

"The operator told me they haven't a new phone."

"Let me worry about that," he said smugly.

I stood up. "Guess that's about all then."

He nodded and got to his feet with a big effort. "I'll call you the first thing in the morning, let you know what I find out."

"You said before something about the case looking helpless, or might look that way. What does that mean?"

"I think your Miss Fulton has probably sold the child."

"Sold it?"

"Rather common practice for unwed mothers these days. You mentioned her landlady thought Miss Fulton was in touch with a lawyer—he'd probably handle it. There's been a great demand for children since the war. Couples who lost four or five years out of their lives through the husband being in the army, find themselves childless. Most girls in Miss Fulton's condition are happy to place the child in a good home, have their doctor bills paid, perhaps receive a few hundred to go away and start all over in another town." He gave me that tight smile again. "By starting all over, I mean a job, of course."

"Tell me, if we can skip your corny jokes, is all this legal?"

"Depends on the state. In New York it's pretty hard to do legally. The tougher the local adoption laws, the bigger the grey-market traffic. I trust you notice the nice touch, blackmarket for everything except babies—they become the greymarket. Sometimes these things work out well for all concerned, other times they become an awful mess with the mother trying to reclaim her child years later, or even blackmail."

I stared at a small rug in front of his TV set, tried to trace the design as I thought about this angle. If the kid had a good home and loving parents, all I would have to do was arrange, somehow, that he was provided for later on in life. Maybe work it out some way in which I could see the kid sometimes …

Temple blew his nose a little. "The idea seemed to shock you at first, now you don't mind it. Do you really want to find your child, Mr. Dolsan? Or are you alarmed that the child may be in need?"

"That cold must be traveling to your ears. When I first came in I told you I wanted to find Peggy Fulton and my kid. Okay, this adoption lick is something I didn't expect. How do they work this?"

"Many ways. But keep in mind that the selling of the baby is merely a guess. I could be all wrong. As to how it's worked— when it isn't a racket the girl …"

"There a racket angle in this?"

"Sometimes. There have been such things as baby farms where girls make a practice of having babies as often as possible. There they usually work both ends—shaking down the man who made them pregnant, and then getting a wad for the sale of the kid. When it's done on what we might call a legitimate basis, often the parties involved move to a different state where the adoption laws are less rigid. But that takes time and money. Then again, there can be a quack doctor involved who simplifies things by making out a false birth certificate. Or the new parents take care of the baby and go through a legal adoption with the mother's consent. But that means the would-be parents have to meet certain requirements and if they could have met them, then they would have taken a child through one of the many agencies in the field. By the way, Miss Fulton may have given her child to such an agency, although there would be a record of her having given birth then."

"Shouldn't there be a record someplace, no matter what she did with the child?"

"The question is, where is *someplace?*" Temple said, touching his throat. "And there are ways in which a birth certificate is … I'm afraid I'm talking too much. Not good for my cold. First thing in the morning I'll start on your case, Mr. Dolsan."

I put on my hat and coat. "Try some hot milk and honey, works for me when I have a cold."

"I fancy a decent night's sleep is my best medicine. I'll phone you before ten tomorrow."

I took a cab up to the Towers, thinking Temple was an odd jerk. "I *fancy* a decent night's sleep …" Guy was probably a queer. I wondered if Hemingway had got my card, if he would call.

No sooner did I get into my apartment when the phone rang. It was Matt Blair. "Red, I'm over at a small shindig at the Waldorf. Not a big party, but good food and the guy is a Chicago manufacturer who wants to meet you, goofy over ball players."

"I can't make it, Matt. I'm expecting an important call … baseball business."

"You're harder to see than a sponsor."

"You know how it is, I'm always on the run. I'm … uh … trying to get a line on a switch hitter they say is terrific. Maybe tomorrow night we'll have supper and chew the fat."

"Some fine girls here, Red."

"Sure, but are they switch hitters?" I cornballed as he laughed and hung up.

I watched TV for awhile, then undressed and carried the phone to the tub, ran a hot bath and soaked as I reread a book on the history of Haiti.

At ten I watched the fights and finished a cigar. Either Robert Hemingway didn't get my card or he'd never heard of Peggy Fulton.

I knocked off some milk and crackers, sent down for a morning paper, and around midnight I was reading in bed when the phone rang. I ran into the bathroom and when I answered it a woman's voice with a clipped English accent asked, "Hello? Hello?"

"Peggy!"

"Ah, so you're back. Why can't you leave me alone? When I was in trouble you weren't around. Now leave me alone."

"But Peggy I never knew ...?"

"Why can't you leave me alone?"

"Peggy, there's something I have to see you about, a ..."

"I don't want to see you—ever! Do you understand?"

"But you don't know what I ...?"

"Just leave us alone! Please!"

"Peggy, for the kid's sake, let me see you, tell you about ..."

"No!" She hung up.

CHAPTER FOUR

I SAT on the edge of the tub, sucking on a cold cigar, two different thoughts banging around in my mind. How did Peggy know I was looking for her? And why the brush? Hell, she sounded as if I'd been hounding her.

I considered calling Temple but it was late and what could he do about anything tonight? I'd tell him in the morning. The main thing—Peggy didn't want to see me so she must be okay. Although her voice didn't sound okay, more like she was frightened. Could be she was married and the husband thought it was his kid, then I'd be fouling up the works and no wonder she didn't want to see me.

I forgot about the old lady Andrews and I actually felt relieved. The kid would have a normal upbringing and that would be that. Hell, I could be cockeyed about the kid even being mine, as Alva said. Could be her pregnancy had nothing to do with me and in her letter Peggy meant she wanted to see me about something else? Might have been jammed up over money. Okay, my only play had been to try and now the game was over.

I washed the cigar taste out of my mouth and went to bed. I slept fine till about six in the morning when I awoke—and the quiet of the apartment was a sad lonely thing.

I'd sold myself a quickie, a cheap bill of goods last night. If there was a kid I knew damn well it had to be mine, just as I knew Peggy hadn't slept with anybody but me. And if I had a kid, well, not only could he use a half a million better than any dogs or cats, but I ought to be able to see him, know something about him. It would be strictly a rock play for me to gyp him out of a bundle of folding dough. Even if she was married where did Peggy come off handing me the fast brush? I wasn't out to cause any trouble. Of course she couldn't know that. But there wasn't any reason why I couldn't see her—on the q.t.—set up some sort of trust fund for the kid. And the way she sounded on the phone last night, maybe it was a lousy marriage and the kid would be in a mess ...?

Everything was "maybe" and all the answers were still in finding Peggy. I felt restless, on edge. I put on a sweat suit and stepped out on the terrace, shadow-boxed for ten or fifteen minutes, working up a good sweat in the cold morning air. I took a warm shower and then an ice cold one, jumped out of the tub wide awake.

It still wasn't 7 A.M. and the thought of eating alone in my kitchen seemed pretty miserable, so I put on slacks and a heavy sweater, went downstairs and walked over to Central Park. It was going to be another cold day. I passed the zoo and the little path where they have pony rides for kids, wondered what it would be like to take my kid to the zoo, watch him laugh at the animals, get big-eyed at a pony ride. When he got to be nine or ten I'd take him to the training camp, that would give him a charge, although I wouldn't give a damn if he became a ball player or not.

Laughing aloud I told myself to stop being a sentimental slob, but it made me feel alive. I was hungry and walked across 57th Street, dropped into the first cafeteria. The sight of all the half asleep faces of men and women grabbing a quick breakfast before rushing to some crummy job made me uneasy again. I could go over to Alva's place but it was so early it would look silly.

I hailed a cab and rode back to the Towers. Blair was an early riser. I'd breakfast with him. Only I wasn't up to any bright conversation about sex or the advertising racket.

The doorman who'd turned Carlos away was on duty and as he opened the cab door he said cheerfully, "Up early, Mr. Dolsan."

"I was running in the park. Getting in shape to take you," I said, for some reason enjoying the startled look on his big puss.

I picked up my mail at the desk—an ad, a copy of Sporting News, and an airmail letter forwarded from San Juan. I read the letter in the elevator—some clown who claimed he'd played ball with me in Rochester had a song and dance about wanting to get a line on a 'sensational' second baseman his brother wrote him about back in his hometown. The pitch: He was in a hospital down in Norfolk and would need "about $75 to return home. For fare and a decent second-hand suit." I threw the letter away, I'd become calloused to hard luck stories long ago.

Then as I was making breakfast and feeling jumpy as hell, I wished I'd sent the slob money. Dough didn't mean a thing to me and here was a guy down and out in a hospital, trying to make it home … I went out into the hallway, looked in the basket for the letter but they were so goddamn efficient in this joint, it was gone. I don't know why, but I felt real bad about it.

I made a couple of thick toasted cheese sandwiches and strong coffee, read the Sporting News. I turned on the TV, then turned it off, got my dirty laundry together … and didn't know what to do with myself. At nine thirty I phoned Temple's office. When I didn't get an answer I tried his home. He said, "I was about to phone you, Mr. Dolsan," and his voice was thick. "I'm in bed with a 103 temperature and what seems to be a virus, so excuse my sounding stuffy."

"You sounded pretty stuffy last night, too."

"Did I?" he asked, not getting it.

"Look, reason I called was, Peggy Fulton phoned last night. Thought I ought to tell you about it."

"When did she call?"

"About midnight."

"Why didn't you phone me at once?"

"I figured you needed your sleep."

"I appreciate that, but you should have called me. Sorry but it seems I'll have to keep to my bed today. However, I've found the new address of the Robert Hemingways. I expect to be up and around tomorrow and a day won't make much difference. What did Miss Fulton say, and are you certain it was Miss Fulton?"

"Sure it was her. She said she didn't want to see me. It wasn't much of a conversation. She seemed excited, kept telling me to leave her alone, and hung up. I can't understand why she won't at least see me."

"I doubt if that was Miss Fulton."

"Who else would call? And she—the voice—had the same accent and …"

"Accent makes it easier to disguise a voice. That's probably the Hemingways, they got your card with your phone and are trying to throw you off the track."

"I thought of that, but I signed the card with a phony name and they, that is Peggy, asked for me. The Hemingways wouldn't know my right name." And I couldn't remember if Peggy *had* used my name or not over the phone last night.

"It's up to you, Mr. Dolsan," Temple rasped. "If you're satisfied it was Miss Fulton and she wants you to stay away from her, that ends the case."

"I've decided I still want to find her, at least talk to her. I think she must be married, frightened I'll tip-off her husband. But all I want to do is tell her I only want to help her and the kid. I want you to keep looking."

"I feel that wasn't Miss Fulton talking last night, which makes the Hemingways a sure lead, they must know something about her. Perhaps they have adopted the baby. Tomorrow I'll go up and see …"

"How about me going up now? I could give them that same pitch about an insurance company and a policy, etc. I could make a few inquiries and if nothing comes of it, you can still do whatever you plan tomorrow."

"You might show our hand, Mr. Dolsan. Best we wait till …"

"I'm going nuts, with waiting. Look, Temple, we're not going after criminals or killers. Either they know about Peggy Fulton or they don't. I'll be careful what I say. What harm can I do? They're not going to pack and run even if they get wise to me."

"Let me state it this way, I strongly advise against you're doing it. I don't let my clients tell me how to work, but if you want to go ahead on your own, I can hardly stop you."

"I'll go up and take a look. See what the set-up is before I ask any questions."

"That's up to you. I'm too sick to argue. However, don't represent yourself as a private detective, you can get into a jam doing that. And don't ask around, that would arouse their suspicions, since it would certainly get back to the Hemingways."

"I'll play it smart."

"Perhaps. But since you've already sent them the card, it will at least look logical that you follow up with a visit. Also, if it comes up don't fail to mention Peggy Fulton's call last night. You don't have to go into details, merely say she called. Otherwise, assuming the Hemingways either called or told her to call, they would spot you as a phony if you didn't mention it. And you'll be better off talking too little then talking too much. Call me the minute you leave them."

"Okay."

Temple coughed over the phone. "I won't count this as a day's work, since I am sick, but let me give you one last piece of professional advice—don't go. Wait till tomorrow and let me handle it." He coughed a couple more times, added, "Although I'm sure you won't take my advice."

"That's a smart deduction. What's the address?"

He repeated it twice, spelling out the name of the avenue, told me it was way up in the Pelham end of the Bronx. I told him to try some warm milk and honey for his cold and hung up.

He was right on one thing, the Hemingways must have told Peggy about the postal card, that was why she called. She knew 'Ross' had to be me. That meant they knew where she was. I went out and walked toward the subway, feeling calmer. I got on the Pelham Bay local and as it crawled along, stopping every few seconds at some empty station, I went over my insurance line carefully, to be sure I sounded like the real goods. Since Peggy was a refugee, I'd say we represented an Englishman, or somebody who had died in England. That would make the story sound better.

I got impatient with the subway and I took off some place in the Bronx, walked a few blocks till I stopped a cab, gave him the address.

Not far from the Whitestone Bridge there are a number of large new apartment houses, sort of a project, I guess. The cabbie stopped before one of them, said, "Here ya are, mister."

There were three rows of bells and names in the lobby, but no Hemingway. In fact most of the name plates were empty. I rang a bell marked superintendent and when an answering buzz opened the door, I rode the elevator to the basement. A couple of women were sitting around washing machines and they pointed out the super's apartment. He turned out to be a small, pock-faced man with thick black hair. He was fairly young and the woman sitting at a table farther back in the room, his wife probably, was very small and dainty, a type you see a lot of in Porto Rico—dainty from lack of food. I asked him, "Can you tell me where the Hemingways live? I don't see their name on the bell."

The woman said to him, in Spanish, "When will you get the agent to hurry the nameplate company? Wait, wait, it should not take so much time."

"I told him a dozen times if I told him once," the man said to her, also in Spanish. Then he told me, "It is apartment 4F. Excuse it but for some reason they make big delay with the nameplates."

I asked in Spanish, "Are you from San Juan?"

"Since my mother quit the fields when I was but a baby. You speak Spanish very well."

"I have worked with the Santurce team for several seasons."

His sharp face lit up. "A ball player with the great Santurce team! You would indeed honor me by coming inside."

As I walked in I said, "I'm in a small hurry," and thought I'd already run my mouth too much—as Temple said I would. This super might ask Hemingway about his ball playing friend, to make small talk, and that would be that. I added, "I am in a different business now and would appreciate it if you do not mention to anyone my being a ball player. It might confuse people."

"My friend I am not a man of many words. Olga, this man is from Santurce."

"So I heard," the woman said, showing her bad teeth with a smile. "I have been away from home too many years, it is good to see someone like you."

The man asked, "Were you in Santurce this year?"

"I was there less than a month ago."

"Ah, you are the lucky one. We were about to have coffee, would …?"

"Thank you, but some other time. I am working for a … uh … insurance company and must see Mr. Hemingway on business."

"It is odd you mention his name for only this morning I thought I saw him around here," Olga said. "If it was him it is the first time he has been here in many weeks. The poor woman is alone."

"It is said he has deserted her and the baby. The baby is cute but the wife has much trouble," the man added. "How a father can ..."

"Trouble?" I cut in. "What kind of trouble?"

He hesitated. "I am not one to make gossip grow. But she has many troubles, big ones. Her husband has left her and she seems to have no money. Also ..." He stopped abruptly.

"Nothing you say to me will go against her. This baby, how old is it?"

"It is a very little baby, perhaps a few months," Olga said. "The child has trouble with the eyes. They say it cannot see yet."

The man nodded. "But the woman is very good, always she smiles, has a happy greeting, despite the worry in her eyes."

I asked him, "Mrs. Hemingway, is she a big woman?"

"No, she is small, about the height of my Olga. Only heavier and strong."

I almost grinned—Peggy Fulton and her farm girl's face and body. "Well, I must get going. I am in a hurry as I said. It has been good to know you two."

"We have been delighted to hear your voice. Is it true that there are now many factories and new houses in San Juan?"

"That is what I have been told," I said, waving at the woman and shaking his hand.

"But there are still many out of work, many living in shacks?" he asked, opening the door.

"Still too many. Good day to you both."

Riding the elevator to the fourth floor I wondered what I'd say to Peggy when she opened the door. If her husband had taken a powder, why did she tell me to leave her alone? Or had he found out he wasn't the father, taken off because of that?

There was the sound of a typewriter working which stopped as I rang the bell of 4F. The woman who opened the door wasn't Peggy. She wasn't a glamour gal or a kid, she was a *woman*—at least 30, wearing old tan slacks and a blouse that showed off a stocky figure with solid hips and a firm bosom.

"Yes?" She said it cautiously, her eyes racing over me.

"Mrs. Robert Hemingway?" I said, looking her over again, taking my time now. Her face was plain and on the meaty side, the full lips painted with a light shade of lipstick that didn't try to prove anything. There was a very faint moustache below an ordinary nose, large eyes, and the dull brown hair was cut short, one of those boyish Italian jobs that set off her face nicely. If she had a regular fluffy hair-do, I suddenly thought, it would make her head too big for her short body.

"I'm Mrs. Hemingway." Her voice was smooth and maybe on the husky side. Her eyes were steady—but scared.

"I'm Frank Ross. I sent your husband a card yesterday."

Relief flooded her face. "Oh yes, the Special Delivery," she said and smiled. The smile almost made her a beauty—her mouth was big and lush, and very warm.

"May I come in and talk to you?"

"Certainly." She stepped aside and as I passed there was a good perfume about her, not anything out of a bottle but a warm clean human odor that was sort of exciting.

All the furniture was new and cheap-looking, and said the Hemingways were broke. I had the feeling there was a piece or two missing, the room was a little too bare. Even counting the large new baby carriage against one wall.

The odd part was, even with this crummy a-buck-down-and-a-buck-when-you-catch-me-furniture, the newness of the room,

I suddenly liked it. Somehow it all seemed more like a real home than any room I'd been in the last couple of years. All at once I felt as comfortable here as I ever did in the Towers.

As if to stress the washed-diaper-smell I finally became aware of, a baby cried in another room. She said, "Sit down, Mr. Ross. I'll be right back."

She crossed the room with a sure stride that I liked. I sat on a foam rubber chair and opened my coat, damn near felt like taking it off, then opening my tie and kicking off my shoes.

I tried to snap out of it by taking stock of the room. In one corner a battered portable typewriter sat on an old bridge table and next to it there were several boxes of envelopes. Addressing envelopes is a rough way of making a small buck. And in case I had any doubts about them being broke, on a cheap coffee table near my chair I saw an open cigarette box—all the butts neatly cut in half.

The walls were bare except for two framed Army discharges. One was made out to Robert (NMI) Hemingway, the other to a Ruth Frances Kahn.

She called out from the other room, "I have to change a diaper, take me a minute."

"Mind if I watch? I'm … uh … fond of children."

"Well, if you haven't a cold … come in if you wish."

There were two small bedrooms off the living room, one with just a dresser and a new double bed. The other, the kid's room, was well furnished: A white crib and dresser to match, a bassinet, a play pen, and a linoleum rug on the floor with pictures of animals on it. There were light blue curtains on the window—the only curtained window I'd seen.

The baby was tiny and fat, with a wide face like Mrs. Hemingway. The kid was laying on his back, it's eyes very clear and big and gentle. There was a kind of patient, contented air about the kid as Mrs. Hemingway changed the diapers, slipped on a new little gown then covered the baby with a fancy pink blanket.

"Very cute," I said, making the asinine cooing sounds adults think babies like. "A big buster of a boy."

"I don't change diapers that fast, this is a girl. My Cathy, the world's most beautiful baby."

I wiggled a finger at the baby and Mrs. Hemingway said, "Don't do that. Cathy was born blind." She said it proudly, almost defiantly.

Very brightly I said, "Oh."

She gave the baby a flash of that wonderful smile as she said, "Now my beautiful Cathy is going to sleep until Mama gives her the noon bottle." She dropped the soiled diaper into a pail of water standing beside the dresser, slipped the kid a big kiss.

I followed her back into the living room. She sat on a thin foam rubber-wrought iron leg couch that looked too hard for comfort, pulled one of her half cigarettes out of her blouse pocket, then changed her mind and put it back. For a moment she stared at me, her eyes very frank. I had to look away. I glanced at the army discharges on the wall and for no reason asked, "Were you a WAC?"

She almost jumped, her face went pale. "What? How did you know?"

I nodded at the wall. Relief came over her face and she mumbled—to herself—"I forgot I had them up." Then she said in a louder voice, "Yes, I was a captain. That's where I met Robert. He was a tank driver in Italy."

"Captain? I had a time reaching staff sergeant. As Yogi Berra is supposed to have said, 'I wanted to stay with the men.' " I tried to grin, wondered why I was talking so much. "That's a joke. Not a very good one."

She was staring at me again. Then she let me have that warm smile: her mouth the friendliest lips I'd ever seen. She said, "I've heard that before. My husband is a charter member of the I-could-have-been-an-officer-club. I have your postal card some place. You wrote about a Miss … Woodson …?"

"A Peggy Fulton. I represent an insurance company. One of our … eh … clients died in England, left a small sum to Miss Fulton. I learned through her former landlady that she knew a Mrs. Hemingway in Staten Island. Easy name to remember. Are you related to the writer?"

"You mean is my husband. No. I'm not the Mrs. Hemingway that Miss Fulton may have known."

"A Robert Hemingway lived in Staten Island up till a couple of months ago."

She nodded. "You probably have the correct Robert Hemingway, I suppose. But I only became Mrs. Hemingway nine weeks ago. Bob's first wife died in childbirth, having Cathy. Bob and I had been friends since army days and Cathy needed a mother—so even though it may have been a bit unconventional, we married within a month after his wife's death. Of course I don't know if she ever knew this Miss Fulton."

"Would your husband know?"

"Maybe. I wired him and was going to phone you as soon as he calls me. Bob is a salesman and working southern New Jersey this week."

"I'd appreciate knowing as soon as I can. You see I'm new on this job and want to make a good showing on …"

"You don't look like a detective."

"I'm not exactly a detective. Although just what does a dick look like?" I asked, thinking of Temple.

"Somehow you don't look as though you'd hurt anybody. I guess the movies make me think of all detectives as hard-boiled goons." She stared at me for a moment and this time I looked right back at her. She smiled, sadly I thought. "I'm sorry to stare, Mr. Ross, but your tan attracts me. I'm quite a sun hound in the summer."

"I was working down in Florida up till a few days ago."

"I suppose you must travel around the country a good deal in your line of work?"

"No. But I did in my former job."

"Bet your wife is glad you changed jobs then. I mean, traveling around and the housing shortage being what it is."

"I haven't any wife," I said, wondering why she was making a point of finding out if I was married. And her reaction puzzled me even more; she almost did a double-take.

"You're *not* married?"

"No. is that a crime these days? Why should it surprise you?"

"As the old gag goes, you somehow look married," she said, trying to toss it off as a joke.

"My wife died several years ago."

"I'm sorry."

"Thank you." I wanted to say, "Don't be. It could never be any of your business and Doris is better off dead." It made me think of the time she was sent to a sanitarium while I was overseas and the army actually wanted to discharge me, send me home to take care of her—as if I could. It was hard to convince them she was better off in the institution. They let her out in six months and she got falling-down drunk the first night, or so she wrote me.

Ruth Hemingway fumbled in her blouse for one of her shortie cigarettes again, then gave it up. She said, "Tell me, about this estate the young lady comes into—I think you said she was young, or at least I got that impression."

"I understand Miss Fulton is quite young and very unfond of caged birds."

"Caged birds?"

"She never liked to see birds caged. Perhaps it was symbolic of her life, or something. I am told she spent some time in a concentration camp."

"I once visited a camp in Bavaria shortly after it was liberated. It almost made me ashamed of being alive. But tell me, Mr. Ross, what do you do in a case when you can't locate the party? Does the insurance company keep the money?"

"I don't know. I suppose they keep it on hand, in case the party, like Miss Fulton, shows up within a certain number of years. All I can do is give it a good try."

She stood up. "I hope you find her. Bob should phone in the morning and I'll ask him and call you."

"Do you have a phone? I couldn't get your number."

"No ... that is we're on the waiting list for one. Bob and I have an arrangement whereby he calls me at a drug store booth at a certain time. I'll phone you tomorrow, Mr. Ross."

"Do that." I got up and followed her toward the door. As we passed the discharge papers on the wall, I said, "I was in the army in Italy. Stationed in Bari most of the time."

"Did you ever get to Rome or Florence?"

"Sure."

"Then we might have passed each other on the street."

"No, I would have remembered you."

She waved a stubby hand at me. "I bet. With all those big-breasted and wonderfully beautiful Italian girls. But it's sweet of you to say that ... I didn't think anybody would ever bother to notice me on a street." She held out her hand. "I wish you luck in finding Miss Fulton."

We shook hands and she said, "Your hand is hard and large. What business were you in before this?"

"I was a baseball player."

"Really? Frank Ross. I don't believe I ever heard of you, but I'm just a casual fan. What are you grinning about?"

"Nothing, a private joke," I said. Hell, whenever I told anybody my *real* name I always got that never-heard-of-you line. "I never got far on the diamond. Never above a busher, I guess. Well, I'll hear from you tomorrow, Mrs. Hemingway. See by the discharge paper your name is Ruth. Nice name."

"I'll call you, Mr. Ross," she said, staring at me for a second longer and then her eyes seemed to water and she turned away. I didn't know what to say, so I opened the door.

I walked to the elevator, then tip-toed back to her door like a ham movie dick. She was crying, real deep sobs that made me feel very strange. Then I heard her walk across the room and the sound of the typewriter working.

I tip-toed back to the elevator, rode down to the lobby. There wasn't a cab in sight and I had to walk a long way before I found one. I didn't mind. I wanted to think about Ruth Hemingway.

Why did she marry this Bob? It didn't make sense ... unless she was afraid of ending up an old maid. Okay, maybe she wasn't pretty like a movie queen, still there was something very ... comfortable about her, warm and friendly. Why should she marry a joker a few weeks after his wife dies to nursemaid his kid? That's what it boiled down to, this Bob had hired himself a full time nursemaid via a marriage license. She was even working without pay. The kid in Staten Island said he'd seen Hemingway dressed to kill and here she was watching her pennies, pounding a typewriter for eating money.

She and this Bob must have been carrying a torch since they first met, but then how come the punk had walked out on her, like the super said? He must be a real jerk, leaving her with his kid, without a dime. She looked lonely but then women seem to have a capacity for being lonely. That was crap—nobody had been as lonely as I had these last dozen or so years. Maybe Doris had been real lonely the two years I was overseas. Although did she ever *really* miss me? Did I every mean a damn thing to her? Everything she wanted she kept trying to find in a bottle. The doc told me never to feel guilty about Doris, but I did. Too bad she didn't have the good-natured strength of a Ruth.... I could never imagine a woman like her needing a bottle for a crutch.

All the way downtown, in the cab, I tried not to think of Doris. The many times she had phoned me in the middle of the night from New York, chewing her words slowly and carefully the way a lush does as she said, "Les honey ... I'm afraid I'm crocked. Les, I'm awful drunk.... I need you. I can't walk."

Odd, no matter how juiced she got, she could always remember where the team was playing, reach me long distance.

I'd be a nervous wreck the rest of the night, picturing her passing out in some joint, being robbed, maybe lined-up in an alley, or crashing her Caddy, lying somewhere all bloody and dead.

I was in a lousy mood when I told the cabbie to let me off at Lexington Avenue. I bought a steak and vegetables for supper, remembered I hadn't had lunch, dropped into a bar for a hamburger and a beer. The fat bartender was sore about having to cook so early in the day and then the punk tried to short change me. I gave him a ten-dollar bill and he claimed I gave him a one. It wasn't quite noon yet and the bar was empty. What got me steamed was the slob wrapping a big salt shaker in a handkerchief and daring me to start something.

I feinted with my right and cracked him hard on the wrist with the side of my left hand. He dropped the shaker and started to yell I'd busted his wrist. I suddenly realized what the hell I'd done and took a powder. Once a busher, always a busher.

I walked as fast as I could toward 3rd Avenue, expecting to hear him yelling for the cops. I caught a cab and rode down to 34th Street, walked over to Park and took another cab back to the Towers. I was sweating ... could already see the item in the papers, DODGER SCOUT IN BAR BRAWL! And the next day I'd be an ex-scout. Hell, I'd given up a half a million bucks to remain in baseball and here I'd almost loused myself up over ten bucks.

When I reached the Towers there was a message from the Dodger office to call a Billy Moore at the Hotel New Yorker, and one to phone Alva. I got Alva and he told me, "Red, you remember a small diamond ring Doris had?"

"I never saw her wear any ring. She was always being robbed of rings and stuff when she passed out. Why?"

"Old lady Andrews called. She just remembered the ring and wants it."

"For Christsakes, now, two years after Doris died!"

"You know her crazy whims. Claims she gave it to Doris when she graduated grade school and ..."

"That would be over 20 years ago, what the hell makes her think I'd have it now?"

"Relax, Red, I'll handle her. Oh, another petty matter, she sent somebody over to look at the house. The roof needs repairs— that's a fact, I checked with our agent—and she insists we fix the roof before she takes over the house. Be about five hundred dollars. Okay?"

"Yeah. Tell them to make it nice and smooth, so she can land on her broom stick!"

"I see I'm bothering you at the wrong time. Did Mr. Temple find anything yet?"

"He's sick in bed."

"Temple's a good man, give him a chance. I have to hang up now, Red; how about supper tomorrow?"

"I don't know. Let me call you," I said, too angry to think straight.

As I dialed Temple I was sore as a boil—damn old bag with her roof and lousy ring. I could almost hear her telling Hanns I'd probably hocked the damn thing.

I dialed two wrong numbers before I got Temple. He was still running a temperature and sounded bad. I told him what the super said about the blind baby and Bob Hemingway having taken a powder, added, "Mrs. Hemingway seems like a fine woman but why she took on this nursemaid job for his kid, I don't know."

"Did she mention the first wife's full name, the hospital where she died?"

"No. She merely said it in passing."

"Won't be too difficult to find that out."

"Main thing is to locate the husband, he's the only one knowing anything about Peggy."

"Perhaps. Did you tell her some one claiming to be Miss Fulton had phoned you last night?"

"Look Temple, it *was* Peggy who called! No I didn't mention it, never came up. Temple, I know you're sick, but is there anyway, anything I can do to speed this up? I want to find that kid, and Peggy, as fast as I can," I said, thinking that when I had everything straight with the kid, I'd tell the old bitch about it to her face, would enjoy seeing her explode.

"Mrs. Hemingway may call you tomorrow. Let me know what she says, although it will undoubtedly be a bull story. If I can leave my bed tomorrow I believe I'll find your Miss Fulton."

"Where?"

"I'm not certain at the moment, but I have some pretty clear ideas about where she is."

"Why can't I ...?"

"Mr. Dolsan, all this talk is making me tired."

"Damnit, I want some action. If you know where Peggy ...?"

"I said I *believe* I know where she is. Please, let me do my job. And if I can get some rest now, I'll be up and around tomorrow. Hang up, Mr. Dolsan."

I heard his phone click. I swore at the dead phone, angry because there wasn't a thing I could do about it, not even hire another dick—no point in too many people knowing about things.

I fooled around the place for a few minutes, turning the TV on and off, trying to glance at a magazine. I finally cooled off and called this Moore. When I got him on the phone a hearty voice boomed, "Red, you little muscleman, remember me?"

"Of course Billy," I lied. "How's things?"

"Juicy. Red, this is the first time I've been in New York since I read in Sporting News about you being a scout. Like I says to the wife, first time I'm in the big city I'm going to phone old Red and tip him off to something fat. Boy, let's us have a drink and hear what you're putting down these days while I let you in on a real fielder."

"Fine," I said like I meant it. "When?"

"Now is dandy with me. There's a bar downstairs here in the hotel. How about that?"

"Great. An hour be okay?"

"Got yourself a date, Red old boy!"

The last thing I felt like was meeting this windbag, but that was my job. I smoked a cigar and looked through the magazine, then took a cab down to the New Yorker. We crawled in heavy truck traffic down 7th Avenue. At 38th Street I paid him off and started walking. I was far too restless to sit still.

At 36th I almost walked into a guy blocking the sidewalk as he jockeyed a rack of dresses from the street to the sidewalk. He had his back to me, pushed into me again. I told him to watch it. He told me to take a certain trip to the moon. I saw the side of his face: it was Carlos. Pinning his arms before he could turn around, I told him in Spanish he wasn't fit for shark bait. He tried to twist out of my hands as he yelled my father shared his bed with a female goat. We sort of wrestled and when people stopped to stare. I let go of him. We laughed and shook hands like a couple of kids. It was exactly what I needed, I felt myself unwind.

After a minute of small talk Carlos' brown face got serious as he said, "I am late. Is it not a shame that I bend my back pushing dresses my people will never wear?"

I looked at the dresses, very light blue fluffy dance frocks looking out of place in the raw cold day. "Maybe they're lucky. Well, I don't want to keep you. I'll try to see you before I leave."

"Yes." Carlos hesitated, slipped me a long look, as if weighing something.

"Anything wrong?"

He shrugged, "Les, I feel bad about asking you this for I do not wish you to think I am making what you call in English—a good thing—of our friendship, but can you lend me $200? I assure you it is really a loan that will be paid back in time."

"Sure. And why shouldn't friendship be a good thing?" I said, taking out my check book. "And don't rush to pay it back. To quote another English saying, I'm not hurting. You need more than $200?"

"No, no. I do not need it for myself. Some good friends are in legal trouble and I am trying to get them out of jail."

I wrote out the check and he shook my hand hard and his eyes started to water. He said, "Be assured I shall pay it back, it is truly a debt of honor with me, my friend," and pushed his rack of dresses on down the street.

I laughed at nothing—this was my day to make people cry.

I was a few minutes late entering the bar and I didn't have a chance to wonder how I'd recognize Moore: I'd hardly stepped inside when this well dressed hunk of lard came rushing over, slapped me on the back, joked about my bald noggin, and practically dragged me over to a booth to be introduced to his soggy wife. I didn't remember ever seeing him before in life but after I'd ordered a beer and a Scotch refill for them, I gathered Moore had been a catcher with a Topeka team I once spent a season with, he had lasted exactly a month there and *that* had been the high point in his baseball "career." Moore was talking in high.

"May will tell you, sometimes when I watch the games on TV I wonder if I did the right thing in giving up ball. Don't make players like you and me no more. Still, I've done all right. Got me a nice business out in Hamptonville, that's way out on Long Island, and we have two of the finest kids in this world. We got no kick, have we May?"

May, a little flushed from her second Scotch, squeaked they certainly couldn't complain.

"But I never forgot you, Red. You were sure hell on wheels at first—greatest first baseman since Hal Chase. Mystery to me why you never made the majors. Still married?"

"My wife died a few years ago."

Moore glanced at his wife and I knew Doris must have done her number in Topeka and every time he'd mentioned me he'd mentioned my lush wife. "Tell you what I have for you, Red. We have a small semi-pro league out our way and I give the boys a hand with coaching. There's a lot of migratory workers out in Long Island who follow the crops, pick potatoes out our way during July and August. Last year we were playing Water Mills, usually a sure win, and damn if they haven't got a ringer, colored kid named Leroy in the outfield. This kid beat us singlehanded—tall, rangy kid who hits well and covers ground like a rabbit. I'm not blowing when I say he has the potential of a Willie Mays and he's as strong as Duke Snider. Hits damn good now even though his stance is all wrong, he chokes the bat. You'll have to work on his hitting—but you can't improve this fielding and his throwing arm is terrific. I said to May there's the sweetest prospect I ever seen. Didn't I, May?"

"All Billy talked about was this Leroy," May said. "I was surprised because Billy says there's too much fuss over colored players and …"

"That was last summer, where's Leroy now?" I cut in.

"I got him on ice for you," Moore said, annoyed at his wife. "Let me explain what I meant about the fuss over Negro players. I think it hurts the colored boys to center attention on them. Take Jackie Robinson and his big mouth. If he …"

"If Robinson didn't have so much to say, he might have been the only Negro in the majors," I said.

"Don't get me wrong," Billy said, patting the air with a fat hand. "May shouldn't have said what she did without explaining. I'm no bigot. What I mean is, the special buildup makes people expecting all colored players to be whiz-bangs. Like old Sachel Paige. Instead of saying he was washed up and old, sports writers made you think because he was colored he was still at the top of his form, his …"

I let Billy talk himself out. I saw Paige pitch a whole lot of years ago in a small park in Harlem and it was hard to believe how great he was. In three innings he went through the other team's batting order, pointing toward first, or the infield, or toward third—whenever he was going to make the batter pop out. When the clean-up man came to bat, Sachel pointed to himself and struck the guy out on four straight pitches.

Billy kept on running his mouth and it took a few minutes before he finally got back to Leroy again. He said, "He's all yours,

Red. He turned 18 last summer and was drafted. That's why I figure it could wait till I saw you, instead of writing you. He has another year in the service and he's in Germany right now. I kind of promised him a job driving one of my trucks, so he keeps in touch with me. Nobody else knows about him, I'm handing him to you on a silver platter. Here's his name and army address," Moore said, writing on a business card. "That's me on the other side. Any time you're out our way, look us up. Nobody makes better clam fritters than my May."

"My claim to fame," May said happily.

I pocketed the card and thanked him. "Is he playing any ball in the army?"

"Kid writes he plays all the time but small time stuff, you know, company team. Don't have to worry, I told him I had connections in baseball and he's to sign with nobody unless I tell him to. Serious kid, Red, takes good care of himself. Worth looking at."

I said I'd certainly keep in touch with Leroy and ordered another round and May announced she'd soon be drunk as a goose. I don't mind two-drink drunks. We made a lot of small talk and I said I had a supper date and there was a mild argument over paying the check, Billy's eyes taking in my worn overcoat. I settled it by flashing my thick wallet and assuring him it was all on the Dodgers. It took me another five minutes of bull about the "team in Topeka," before I could get out of there.

It was about six when I picked up an evening paper and reached the Towers, kicked off my shoes, took off my shirt and tie, and started cooking. I found myself thinking of Ruth, wondering why I thought her far more exciting than the call girl, who certainly had it all over her in looks—whatever that is.

I was kind of pooped from running around and the apartment really seemed 'cosy' as I stretched out on the couch, nicely full of food, read the paper.

The phone rang and I knew it was Matt with another screwy party on. It wasn't.

A smooth voice asked, "Mr. Les Dolsan?"

"Yeah," I said hoping it wasn't another tip: I had my share for the day.

"I'm speaking for Peggy Fulton. I'm her lawyer."

"Where is she?"

"That happens to be none of your business. She knows you're trying to locate her and she wants to be left alone. You've caused her enough misery, so ..."

"How does she know I'm looking for her?" I cut in. "And what's your name?"

"My name is Wagner. Mr. Dolsan, this is a friendly call, let us not play games. You are looking for her. She phoned you last night and begged you to stop, but we know you haven't. You might call this a warning—you're in rather a bad spot. I'm certain you do not wish to be involved in the resulting publicity an arrest for bastardy and rape would cause."

"Rape?"

"Legal rape—Peggy was under 18 when she spent the night with you."

"You're threatening the wrong joker," I said, putting up a front. But for all I knew she could have been under age. After all, I barely knew her name, much less her age."

Wagner said in a patient mild voice, "I am not threatening you, Mr. Dolsan, merely pointing out your precarious position. Peggy doesn't wish any trouble either. My sole interest in calling you is to prevent trouble. Miss Fulton is happy and comfortable, her only worry is that you'll show up."

"You mean she's married?"

"I'm not at liberty to say. The less you know the better. All I can tell you is that both she and the boy are fine. However, if you persist in tracking her down, you'll cause a great deal of unhappiness for both of them. In that case, we'll throw the book at you."

"Well, I was only looking in order to help her," I said.

"In that case you can stop looking, Mrs.… uh … Miss Fulton doesn't need any help. I want you to know I have a tape of your conversation with her last night, and an affidavit along with her birth certificate. She has placed this matter entirely in my hands. You don't know what trouble really is until you try to contact her again. By again I mean not next month or next year—never. Is that understood?"

"Why doesn't she come and tell me all this?"

"It should be obvious she hates you and that also she's not in any position to ever see you."

"Look, you said this was a friendly conversation. Okay, if she's married I'm not out to cause any trouble. But I must see her."

"Why?" The voice grew tough.

"Well, there's some money involved," I said, hesitating.

"She hasn't got a dime."

"You misunderstand. I feel a certain responsibility towards the boy and I'd like to arrange to set up a small trust fund. I could arrange this with Peggy without any embarrassment."

"I'll ask her about this. Of course such a fund would not give you the right to ever see the boy, or Peggy again."

"That's okay. All I want is to see Peggy, any way she wishes to arrange such a meeting, work out a trust fund, and that will be the end of it."

"I doubt if she'll chance it. Once you find her you might try to get the boy and …"

"You just told me the charges you can toss at me, I'm not looking for trouble. I have some money and might as well help the boy."

"All I can do is ask her. You understand, whether she accepts the money or not, you agree to leave her alone—forever."

"Yes, but I'd rather have her tell me that."

"That's up to Mrs.... to Peggy to decide. I'll phone you this time tomorrow night, let you know her decision. And let me say, Mr. Dolsan, I'm glad we've reached an adult approach to things. Good night, sir."

I hung up and sat there for a moment, thinking. This Wagner hadn't been so shrewd, he'd let 'Mrs.' slip a couple times. Okay, Peggy was married: I'd tried to do the right thing, perhaps I still could fix the kid up with ten or twenty grand. At least I tried, my conscience was clear.

As I lit a cigar I felt both relieved and a little sorry—sorry I couldn't put the boot to old lady Andrews. Still, if I could just see Peggy I might get her to work out something. Maybe divorce her husband and go through the legal business of marrying me and having me adopt the kid, then we could divorce. It was all a little crazy and God knows what her husband would say ... but for a half a million bucks a lot of people will stand very still.

CHAPTER FIVE

I DECIDED to call Temple, I had a new idea on things. When I got him on the phone his voice sounded better. He said, "I had the doctor in, gave me an injection that broke the fever. With a good night's sleep I expect to be working tomorrow on your case."

"There's a new angle I want you to work on," I said and told him about the lawyer's call. I ended with, "What I want you to do is this, either see if you can trace this Wagner and through tailing him get to Peggy, or I thought if she does come to see me tomorrow or the next day, you could shadow her. You see, even though she is married, I want to have a chance to talk to her alone. Get this money thing settled for sure," I added weakly, not wanting to tell him about the will. There was silence on the phone and I asked, "What do you think?"

"Dolsan, I think you're a prize horse's ass!"

"That's nice to hear. Of course I've had guys tell me that for nothing instead of for fifty a day."

"What are you paying me for? Why did you have to talk all over your face to this lawyer? Handling him is my job."

"What was I supposed to do? The fellow called me, I couldn't hang up on him. I don't see what you're up in the air about."

"All you did was put yourself in a blackmail swindle!" Temple said loudly. "A lawyer named Wagner, what's his full name, is he a New York City lawyer, a New Jersey attorney, or what?"

"I don't know."

"Why don't you find out who you're talking to before spilling everything!"

"Cut the ball of fire act, Temple. What did I spill? Sure I said something about money. I didn't want to lose contact with the guy and I do want to set up a trust fund. If Peggy is happy, I'll establish a fund and that will be that."

" 'That will be that' is a cute phrase, till you find out what *that* means. How much did you offer him?"

"You mean how big a trust fund? I don't think I mentioned any amount but I was figuring on about twenty thousand."

"Can you afford to throw away twenty thousand, Mr. Dolsan? I always thought ball players were underpaid."

"I'm not throwing it away, and if you must know I can afford it. Don't worry, before I hand out a cent I'll have my lawyer check and double check everything."

"And if it's all a swindle, what will you do, run to the D.A.? Let the whole mess break in the papers? Mr. Hanns said you wished to avoid publicity on this."

"Don't jump the gun, Temple. I told you he didn't ask for money, I was the one suggested it."

"Know what will happen now? He'll call tomorrow and say Miss Fulton wishes a fund set up but when it comes to signing any papers, you'll never see her. Wagner will hand you a cock and bull story about her being sick or out of town or.... Wait a minute, did he call you Ross or Dolsan?"

"Dolsan. He said Lester Dolsan."

"I don't see how he could have known your name."

"Obviously Peggy told him."

"No, I don't think Miss Fulton told him a thing, but somebody else did. You see if he used the name Ross, it would be logical, he got it from that card you sent the Hemingways. Listen to me carefully, Dolsan, perhaps being boon-buddys with everybody is part of your job as a baseball scout, but you talk too damn much. Up to now we were looking for Miss Fulton on *our* terms, now somebody has moved in on us. No one even knew you were searching for Miss Fulton except your friend Blair, Mr. Hanns, the landlady, and the Hemingways. One of them has been in touch with this shyster, put him ...”

“One other person knew—you.”

There was a moment of silence on the phone. I had the feeling Temple was grinning at the other end. “That’s the first intelligent thing you’ve said tonight. By all means, don’t rule me out. I’ll return your check in the morning and ...”

“Don’t gas your huff, Temple. You named a couple of good friends of mine. You want to be ‘logical,’ okay, I completed the list. I want you to keep on the case, but the important thing now is to locate Peggy, so I’ll have a chance to talk to her alone, without any lawyers or husbands around. I have to talk to her.”

“Why alone?”

“To arrange this fund business. Way I see it, I’ll hear from Wagner and he’ll set-up a meeting with Peggy. By shadowing her, or Wagner, you should be able to locate Peggy.”

“I’m certain I can find Miss Fulton by tomorrow afternoon. Mr. Dolsan I’ll stay on the case if from here on in you do as I say. You like the movies?”

“What?”

“Tomorrow morning go to a ten o’clock Broadway movie. When you come out, call my office. Then go in and see another show and call me again. Keep doing that till you hear from me. May hurt your eyes but it will at least keep you out of trouble. And take my word for it, you’re getting involved in a bad mess.”

“But Ruth—Mrs. Hemingway is to call me in the morning? And what about Wagner’s call?”

"Don't worry, if they don't reach you, they'll keep calling. This trust fund is a sweet piece of bait. Now you may get another call from Miss Fulton tonight—which I'm certain will be a phony. But if she should call, play it straight, say the lawyer called and everything is okay. And if she should phone tonight, try to talk as little as possible, then call me at once, no matter what the time. Understand?"

"Yes but ... I have the feeling this Wagner is on the level. Suppose he is? I don't want to lose all contact with Peggy."

"He'll keep calling. If I'm wrong and this isn't a swindle, he'll certainly keep calling. Nobody expects you to hang around your apartment all day awaiting a phone call. But keep one thing in mind, stop telling people about Peggy Fulton!"

"Okay, you're the detective."

"Thank you for remembering that," Temple said sarcastically. "Now tomorrow, you keep going to the movies and calling my office till you reach me. Agreed?"

I said yes and we hung up. Temple was right about one thing—how did Peggy know I was looking for her? Unless Ruth told her, I couldn't picture Blair, or certainly not Hanns, saying anything. I wrote this Leroy over in Germany, telling him to be sure and get in touch with me at the Dodger office whenever he got out of the army, that I was a friend of Billy Moore's.... I'm pretty good at writing the kind of letter that doesn't arouse too much hope in a kid.

I found a paperback book on flying saucers in the bookcase, soaked in a hot tub and skipped through the book. Now and then I thought about Wagner, certain Temple was wrong. For one thing, he sounded like a nice guy, although that didn't mean a damn thing. But damn if I did get into a swindle—I'd sure have to pay through the nose—any kind of a stink in the papers and I'd be lucky to even get a job as water boy with one of those semi-pro Canadian teams always advertising for players.

About eleven o'clock as I was laying in bed, trying to finish the book, the phone rang. I reached for it, then stopped. If this was Peggy I had to get her to listen to me, agree to see me, get through to her that I wasn't out to rook or hurt her. But I had no idea how I could do it.

I picked up the receiver and an odd voice, kind of high for a man, asked "Red Dolsan?"

"Yeah."

"Red, you drove Doris to drink and suicide, are you trying to drive Peggy out of her mind too?" The voice was almost a nasal whine.

"Who ... who is this?" I asked, choking on the words.

"Does that matter? Forget Peggy Fulton, unless you want to find another body in the bath tub. Is that what you want, Red? *Is it?*" There was sudden harshness to the voice that cut straight into my brain.

An icy hand seemed to grab my guts, twist them till my heart was about to explode, I was too numb to talk.

"Red, are you there?" The voice was a shrill whine again. "Leave Peggy alone or you'll make her end up like Doris did. Forget Peggy, or you'll kill her too!"

The click of his hanging up seemed to rush at me over the wire, club me. It took a long time before I was able to move ... drop the receiver back in the cradle ... I hadn't taken a jolt like this in years.

"Goddamn you, you miserable son-of-a-bitch!" I thought and suddenly the bedroom was full of noise and I realized I was screaming the words. That brought me up short and I walked around the room, trying to think. Nobody knew about Doris killing herself except Hanns. Blair knew she died but not about being a suicide, the bloody tub. What lousy rat would accuse me of such a thing? It couldn't be Hanns, but who else?

I was almost running up and down the room, trembling with rage, my head splitting. I considered going to see Hanns but in my mood I might beat his head in. And it couldn't be Alva, it didn't make sense. I sure wasn't going to call Temple, have to explain Doris to him.

But if it wasn't Alva, who else knew? There had been a piece in the Canadian papers at the time, maybe even in the U.S. papers, but that was years ago. It couldn't be Blair or ...

It had to be the old witch! Sure, be like her to start needling me now. She was just crazy enough to hire somebody to call, drive me nuts. It figured, she was sore at seeing me, at the settlement of the will ... and she was crazy enough to do any ...

The phone rang.

I picked it up and didn't make a sound. The same high voice said, "Red, if Peggy cuts her wrist, she'll leave a note. You won't get off lightly this time. Maybe she'll take the baby with her. Leave her alone, Red, leave her alone ... don't make her another Doris...."

I slammed the receiver down, ran to the bathroom and got sick. It *had* to be that old bitch! But my God, how did she know about Peggy, about the kid? Maybe she had hired a dick, too? Maybe ...? Hell, it *had* to be her.

I started pacing up and down the bathroom, my head throbbing. I heard the phone ring again and didn't answer it but the ringing seemed to jab at my head. When it stopped, I grabbed the phone directory, called the nearest store and told them to send over a pint of 100 proof rye and make it fast. I'd used booze as a medicine a few times before.

I stared out at the lights of the city from the terrace doors, feeling myself going to pieces. I'd damn near cracked when Doris killed herself and it took a lot of couch talk to snap me out of it. Now … the phone rang again and I covered it with a pillow, as if strangling it. I was cursing and crying and then the bell rang.

I ran to the door, took the bottle and threw a ten dollar bill at the delivery man. Sitting on the bed I drank the pint in three big gulps, pouring it down my throat, fighting back the desire to throw up. I heard the phone ring and even managed to stand and place the empty bottle neatly on the floor before I passed out.

CHAPTER SIX

THE CLOCK claimed it was 9 A.M. I sat up in bed and didn't feel hungover: I didn't feel anything—not even alive. I went to the bathroom like a robot and had a hot bath and came to under a cold shower.

As I shaved I suddenly felt pretty good, decided to dismiss last night from my mind. It was a trick I mastered with Doris. When she'd phone me long distance that she was half-crocked, I would try to convince her to go back to the apartment and get some sleep. Then I'd start worrying the rest of the night whether she did or not. The only way I could keep myself from going nuts was to cut the entire incident from my mind, pretend it never happened. I had plenty of practice at doing it and I did it now. It was because of Doris' calls I never shared a room on the road, always paid for my own room. It didn't make for good feeling on the team.

I even felt better after stuffing myself with French toast and strong coffee. Slipping on an overcoat I went out on the terrace and watched the city below, seeing nothing. I was in one of those moods—and trying like hell to stay with it—where you feel everything will work out all right and the world isn't such a bad ball after all. Of course, back in my mind there was one thought lurking—last night had been the work of Mrs. Andrews and no matter what I'd get back at her.

But there hadn't been any last night. Period. Even when I threw the empty bottle away, took the pillow off the phone, I felt okay. Nor did I feel excited when the phone rang. It was Carlos.

"Red, my friend, I try to call you before but no answer."

"I was out getting breakfast," I lied. "What's new?"

"I call you because yesterday when we part, and thanks again for the loan, a man stop me on the street. He ask if that wasn't Herb Jones I was just talking to. I tell him you are Red Dolsan, the baseball player. So he say excuse him he thought it was his old friend Mr. Jones. Then he say he never heard of you as a ball player. We talk some more and then I get idea he is pumping me for information, so I leave. Maybe I have wrong feeling about all this, but I think I should tell you."

"What did he look like?"

"Pretty tall, about six feet, maybe 35 or 40 years old. Real North American, dressed good. Looked like a man eating regularly. Tell you, my friend, he did not strike me as detective. He was most polite. All this took maybe two three minutes but later it give me funny feeling, Red, you in any trouble?"

"No." I wondered if this guy could be the private dick the old bitch must have hired to tail me. But then what could he get from Carlos? Still, if he'd seen me give Carlos money he might have become interested—if he was tailing me.

"My friend, are you there?"

"Yeah. Carlos, if you ever see this guy again, call me at once. Now don't try anything, like following him or slugging him, just call me and tell me where he is, if you can."

"I will do that. The ..." The operator asked for five cents more and I heard Carlos cursing gently in Spanish, then he said, "I am out of nickels. But I will phone you the second I see this man again."

The operator's impersonal voice cut in again. I started to ask his number, to call him back, but he shouted a fast good-bye and we were cut off.

As I was dressing and wondering if the guy could mean anything, the bell rang, and Matt stood there in a silk bathrobe, looking pale and shot.

"Red, I know you keep something in your refrigerator beside ice cubes and tonic. Can you let me have a glass of milk?"

I said sure and for a split second I pictured Matt as the bastard on the other end of the phone last night. But the idea was silly. It had to be Mrs. Andrews' lousy work.

In the kitchen he drank the milk slowly, belching a little. "I don't know Red, I seem to be drinking too damn much lately. Not merely the night time elbow bending either. All day long somebody is either offering me Scotch or a Bloody Mary, or I'm tilting my own bottle for them. Too much acid, gives me belly pains."

"Have you seen a doc?"

"I'll try milk for a few days. Make myself take two quarts a day."

"You'll get the runs. See a doc and play it safe."

He shook his head. "Only as a last resort. It's a matter of principle with me."

"You a Christian Scientist now?"

"No. I've always considered myself a little above the Madison Avenue maze. Advertising is an exciting way of making a big buck but you can get swamped in it too. Now if a doc should tell me I have a charcoal-grey ulcer, which I think I have, I'd feel … trapped. That's why I'm giving myself a week on the milk wagon. How's the ivory hunting?"

"Lucked up on a few prospects while hanging around the house."

Matt sighed. "If I had sense I'd have taken a week off and gone down to Vero Beach with you. Must be terrific."

"It isn't. It's too big, too much noise and tension. Most times I feel lost, so many people I don't know. Sure there's a few old timers hanging around for kicks and because they don't know what to do with themselves. And the regular members of the squad, most of them soft and overweight, trying like mad at the last minute to diet—and weakening themselves. Then there's the kids on the farm teams, all trying like hell and maybe finally realizing they don't have it. Different when you travel with a team …"

The phone rang. I thought of last night and got a chill as I said hello. Ruth asked, "Mr. Ross?"

"Good morning, Ruth." I didn't want to say her last name in front of Blair.

"Didn't think you'd recognize my voice."

"You have an interesting voice."

"Well thank you. I left Cathy asleep to make this call so I'll have to make it short. I spoke to Bob a few minutes ago. He doesn't remember his wife ever mentioning any Peggy Fulton. I'm sorry we can't be more useful."

"That's all right. Thanks for trying."

"I hope you find her. Good-bye, Mr. Ross."

"Thanks for calling, Ruth."

"Luck." She hung up.

As I put the phone down Matt asked, "Scouting for a girl's team now? No wonder I haven't been able to get you to a party. Young? Stacked?"

"Let's call her mature. As for being stacked, I haven't been able to find out."

"Better make fast time, you'll be leaving in a week or so."

Matt had another glass of milk while he told me of his current sex problem, his ex-wife again, and when he finally left I went downstairs. I picked up my mail, all ads which I threw away, and walked out.

It was early and I didn't know what to do with myself. I sure wasn't going to hang around the house, waiting for any more of last night's phone calls. Temple's idea about going to the movies—that was silly. Not only can't I take the pap they put on the screen, but I felt too lonely and restless to sit still.

Walking uptown I considered seeing the old witch and having things out with her, but what good would that do, I couldn't prove she had hired anybody to make the calls. And the damn will hadn't been probated yet, was just going through the courts, so if I stirred her up now, I'd be back where I started.

I kept walking along aimlessly, but all the time knowing what I felt like doing—I wanted to see Ruth Hemingway. For no special reason—I simply felt like seeing her. At 86th Street I took a cab up to her place.

I didn't get any answer when I rang her bell, couldn't hear a sound. I was real disappointed until I rode the elevator to the basement and Olga told me Ruth usually took the kid for an airing on the other side of the houses where there was a park of sorts.

When I saw her it gave me a bang: she was bundled up in a worn blue coat topped by a red beret, and black slacks, as she pushed the carriage along. Although the nip in the air put a healthy red on her cheeks, there were tired hollows under her eyes. Probably up all night batting out those crummy envelopes.

She was so startled she actually jumped when she first saw me. Then the warm smile and, "Mr. Ross! In the neighborhood on another case?"

I'd been kind of asking myself *why* I wanted to see her again and now I knew—it was the smile. I said, "Nope. I came up to see you. Had some time to kill, thought we'd talk some more."

"About that Miss Fulton? I told you …?"

"Nope, just talk. Do you mind, Ruth?"

"Certainly not. Although I hardly know if this is flattering or not to a woman still on her honeymoon."

Some honeymoon, I thought, wondering again why she took all this crap from Hemingway.

She stared at me for a second, said, "You know I believe you did come up just to talk to me. There's something about you ... your face ... that's rugged and honest and ..."

"And ugly," I added.

"They'd never mistake you for Robert Taylor but I think you're better looking than any movie star—your face isn't weak or shallow."

"Truth is I think you're pretty too," I said, trying to make it sound like a joke. For a moment we walked down the street in silence, except for the jingling of some plastic rattles hanging from the top of the carriage. The baby was sleeping under a pink blanket. "What's the kid's name again?"

"Cathy."

"You know to look at her, never tell she can't see."

"Seeing doesn't make much difference to a baby at this age. But when she starts walking, then it will be a little rough."

"Any chance of her ever seeing?"

"Not unless science learns a great deal more about eyes in the next dozen years. But I have faith that before Cathy becomes a young lady the doctors will be able to help her. That is some days I have faith—and some days I feel disheartened. The eyes are the last part of the body to form and Cathy was a premature child, spent her first month in an incubator. Only in the last year or so that doctors have been able to keep premature babies alive at all, and they don't know much about it. They call this blindness *retrolental fibroplasia*. In plain English it means there was too much oxygen in the incubator and it destroyed the eye tissues. Seems a terribly stupid reason for a person to go through life sightless, but we must realize science is learning all the time. When I get bitter I thank God Cathy is alive."

"You've taken on a large job, raising somebody else's baby and …"

Ruth said sharply, "Don't ever say that, Frank. I don't mind talking about her lack of sight. It's a fact I can't forget or ignore. But this *isn't* somebody else's baby, Cathy is mine! Shes' the only baby I'll ever have. Her blindness may turn out a handicap but we all have some handicap or another. It also means I'll love her with more than ordinary mother love, that we'll have a closer relationship all our lives."

"Never thought of that last angle, but it's still a big job you've taken on."

"This is *my* child—it's a way of living, not a job. And I like it!"

"Sorry, I didn't mean to speak out of turn."

"Nothing to be sorry about and don't feel sorry for me. If you don't mind, let's talk about something else, Mr.…. Frank. Tell me about your being a ball player. With what team?"

"Teams, not team. I've played a lot of ball—guess you could call me a has been that never was. I warmed the bench for the Cards for part of a summer, and before the war I was brought up from a farm club to play the last few weeks of the season with the Giants. I've bobbed around in about every minor league and association out. I even played ball down in the Mexican League for the Pasquels. Every time I had what is laughingly known as my big chance, I fluffed it, turned out to be a busher. Of course now I'm too old to play, but baseball is still about all I know."

"Is that where you got your tan, playing ball?"

"Yeah, I was doing some part-time ivory hunting-scouting— before this insurance job turned up," I lied, telling myself I was talking too damn much. "I like to be near the game—suppose if there wasn't any other way I'd sell peanuts in a ball park."

"It doesn't sound dull. You must have traveled a great deal. I love to travel."

"Used to give me a charge, at first, but you get damn sick of hotels and stool-joints, living in a suitcase. After awhile you find out a dugout is a dugout whether it's in the Yankee Stadium or in the Class D League. Thing that eats me up, or used to, was the idea I really had the goods. It may sound like bragging but I was a hell of a first baseman. When I first came up I was one of these brash, tough studs, cocky and pushing. I lived and slept baseball, and I was good at it, the only exit for me from being poor."

"But ...?" Ruth said with mild sarcasm.

"I got married."

"And that was bad? I thought most ball players were married?"

I didn't know whether she was making fun of me or not, but for some reason—maybe because of the phone calls last night, or maybe because I felt so at ease with her—the words kept gushing out and I told her everything about Doris, except I used a different name. I even told her about finding Doris in the pink water of the tub, her wrists slashed. I was so full of myself I didn't realize we'd stopped walking and were standing in front of a new supermarket. I held up my hands in mock surrender. "Why didn't you shut me off? I've been running my mouth like a nervous breakdown."

Ruth looked a little startled for a split second, as though I'd said something out of the way, then the wonderful smile and, "I'm glad you talked, now I feel like we're old friends. That's what struck me yesterday, the loneliness your face shows. You see I know a bit about loneliness myself ... and about breakdowns too. Your wife really put you through a ringer."

"Perhaps it was a self-made wringer. But I went into a kind of nose-dive after she killed herself—put in time on the couch. I don't have much confidence in these head docs and analysts, but at least they shook me loose from the idea it was all my fault," I said, thinking how I'd damn near forgotten all that last night.

"How could you ever blame yourself after the way she self-ishly ruined your career?" Ruth asked, the anger in her voice making it sound exciting.

"Honey, no matter what they may tell themselves the only *real* reason a person drinks heavily is because they're unhappy, have to escape from themselves. Going on a real toot day after day is physical torture. How much worse can you feel than a bad hang-over? So you don't take on that pain without a reason. My wife was unhappy. I used to rake our life over in my mind, trying to see where I'd made her unhappy. We started off all wrong: When we first met I was a dumb farm boy, and to me she seemed the height of sophistication. When she rode the bottle I thought it was smart, 'society' stuff. Sounds crazy now, but that's how simple I was then. Another thing, for a long time I worshipped her. That's not the way a marriage should be either. Maybe that's why I felt guilty, I was so nuts about her. But then I began to hate her, felt goddamn sorry for her, and it dragged along like that for years and years. She must have known. Not that I had other women, the thing was we had nothing. The point I'm trying to make is, after she died the head docs convinced me alcoholism is as much a disease as TB, and she was sick long before she ever knew me. Look, I've run my gums enough. Want me to watch Cathy while you shop?"

"She'll be all right out here and she needs the air. Come in. I'll let you push my shopping cart around."

It didn't take her long to shop. She bought milk, a few eggs, three jars of baby-food, yesterday's bread, and a pound of the cheapest meat—breast of lamb. I could see her adding it up as she went along. She spent $1.19. I carried the bag outside and care-fully put it in the carriage, asked, "Want me to push?"

"Thanks but I like the exercise."

We walked along and I suddenly remembered I hadn't phoned Temple. I went through the routine of slapping my pockets, said,

"I'm out of butts. You keep walking slowly, I'll catch up. What brand do you smoke?"

"I have cigarettes home."

"But I need some. I'll be right back."

I ran to the store and filled one of the wire carts with a steak, a smoked tongue, three large canned hams, a couple dozen jars of baby food, cans of frozen juices, rice, flour, soap powder, and any canned stuff I saw. At the cashier's desk I added a carton of every brand cigarettes they had. While he was adding things up, I went to a wall phone and called Temple's office. I gave my name to the girl who answered and she said, "Mr. Temple isn't in yet, Mr. Dolsan, but he left a message that you are to keep calling here every few hours."

I thanked her and went back to the cashier. The tab was $42.69 and I paid, gave them Ruth's address and they said they'd be downright happy to deliver it.

I could see Ruth wheeling the carriage a few blocks away and I jogged after her. When I reached her she gave me that warm smile, asked, "What were you doing, growing the tobacco?"

"Sorry I took so long but …"

"Don't keep saying you're sorry. I don't like to hear that word. I'm out for the air, another five or ten minutes doesn't matter."

"I made a phone call, got hung up."

"My, are puns one of your talents too?"

I looked at her, wondering what she was talking about. She smiled again. "I'll take one of your cigarettes."

"I'm sor … Look, I talked so much on the phone I forgot about the butts. I'll run back and get you a pack."

"Oh stop it. We'll be home soon and I'll get a smoke. You're fine for my ego, Frank. Nobody has paid this much attention to me since I was 18."

"Doesn't your husband pay any attention to you?"

"Of course," she said too quickly. "Even though we're newly-weds, Bob and I have been friends for years and the fine edge, the little foolish gestures have worn off and … Lord, why am I trying to explain this?"

"Also his job seems to keep him away from you. That must be a hell of a good job."

"A job's a job," she said, blushing slightly. "Mr. Ross, what are you feeding me?"

I laughed it off without answering, wondering what I was feeding myself. In my old age I suddenly became the boy with the fast line. We walked the rest of the way in silence. I helped her in with the carriage and they sure make baby carriages damn heavy these days. When we got out of the elevator and she was unlocking the door, she asked, "Could you stand a cup of tea after all that cold air?"

"Sure thing."

"Let me take care of Cathy, get her in the crib. I'll be with you in a few minutes."

I took off my coat, got a cigar working—like I was right at home.

Ruth came out of the baby's room wearing a red turtleneck sweater that set off her solid figure. The sweater, the slacks, the close-cut hair; she should have looked a little on the mannish side. But on Ruth it all seemed to frame and heighten the sultry quality of her face. As she walked into the kitchen she said, "I'll have tea on in a moment. I hope I have a few cookies around some place."

I had about finished my rope when she brought out the tea and some stale hard cookies shaped like animals. They tasted better than they looked. For some reason we started bulling about Italy. She'd been with the 15th Army and we shot the breeze about Leghorn and Naples, Lake Garda and Milan.

As she took out one of her half-cigarettes, lit it, and told me, "I do this because I'm trying to cut down on smoking, think there's a lot to this lung cancer theory …" the doorbell rang.

For a silly moment I thought it was her husband. She opened the door and two grocery clerks were each holding a large box of food. I'd forgotten all about the groceries. One of the clerks said, "Mrs. Hemingway?"

"Yes."

"Here's your order. Say, excuse me, but are you related to …?"

"No. What order? I never ordered all this …"

One of the guys looked at a slip as he said, "Says here, Mrs. Hemingway and apartment number …"

"He ordered it," the other guy said, jerking a fat thumb at me. "All paid for."

She turned to me, her face burning. "What's the idea, Mr. Ross?"

"No idea," I told her. "Fellows, leave it on the kitchen table."

There was a heavy silence in the room till I gave them a buck to split on their way out and when she closed the door Ruth asked coldly, "Will you explain this, Mr. Ross?"

"Nothing to explain, Ruth. I merely thought you could use the … uh … things. That's all there is to it."

"I consider it a rude and crude gesture, a …"

"Maybe it is, but don't take it so big. You said before we're friends. I wasn't grandstanding, just being friendly. I'm sure if you thought I was hungry you'd invite me in for a bite without thinking about it."

"Of all the gall! I'm not broke or hungry! I'm …"

"I know." I cut in, sore—at myself for making this rock play with the groceries, "You told me, you're smoking those two-for-one cigarettes to break the habit."

I stood up. We were facing each other and she said slowly, "I look upon this as a cruel and ..."

"Okay, okay, I'm sorry. I didn't mean it to be cruel or anything but ... well, I just felt like doing it."

"You can take all those boxes out with you!"

I was embarrassed and I was angry. I let her have it—hard. "Come off it, Ruth. Of course you're not broke, you're typing those lousy envelopes for the exercise! You buy the cheapest foods in the store because you left your salting money home! You haven't any curtains or enough furniture in this room because you like things that way. And that wonderful clown you married, the one whose 'foolish gestures have worn off,' he isn't typing envelopes for a few bucks, he's walking around dressed to kill. But then how would you know, he took a powder soon as he was sure he had a built-in nurse for his kid!"

The red in her face drained to the palest white I've ever seen and she said in a low voice that could have cut me to shreds, "So you *have* been snooping around! That's a filthy thing to do, aside from the fact all this is absolutely none of your business!"

She seemed ready to swing on me. I got my coat and stopped at the door. "For the records I haven't been snooping, I ... uh ... What difference does it make? You're right, this isn't any of my business. As for the food, I certainly didn't mean it the way you think. I only meant to ... I don't know now what the hell I meant now! I'm sorry. Good-day."

I practically ran out of the apartment, didn't wait for the elevator, trotted down the stairs. I walked for over an hour, until I reached Manhattan. I knew I'd made a horse's rear out of myself with Ruth and I didn't know why. I'd never been much of a chaser, and Ruth was about the last thing I could imagine myself going for. In Havana and San Juan I'd lived with girls who were so young and beautiful you were suddenly glad you were alive to even look at them.

When I reached upper Manhattan I took a subway down to the Towers, tossed off my clothes and sat in a hot tub, reading about flying saucers. Along about five I dressed and made supper, remembered Temple. When I phoned his office his secretary told me, "I've been waiting for your call, Mr. Dolan. Mr. Temple wants you to wait at your apartment. He'll either phone or drop in to see you shortly."

"I'm there now. Sorry I made you wait."

I had about put the receiver back in its cradle when the phone rang again and the same nasal voice from last night said, "You insist upon hunting Peggy down, killing her, don't you, Dolsan? Like to know what bar she's in now? What ...?"

It still hit me hard but it didn't floor me like last night. My voice was loud and harsh as I cut in with, "Tell the old biddy it won't work!" and slammed the phone down.

I walked around the room slowly, then turned on the TV and stared at some 'kids' comic' making an ass of himself—without seeing him. I was full of a slow rage, thinking all sorts of childish things—like how I'd have the old lady squirming at my feet and tell her to go to hell ... that she was broken and in rags and really needed the half a million and I still told her to go to hell. The TV show changed to a brassy band and that made me snap out of things.

I was surprised and glad I hadn't been too upset, but one thing was for sure ... I had to find that kid, take the dough away from the old witch.

The phone rang again and I jumped. But it was the house phone this time. A clear man's voice asked, "Mr. L. Dolsan?"

"Talking."

"My name is Phil Preston. I'm down in the lobby. I'd like to talk to you. I'm Peggy Fulton's husband."

"Well ... let's talk. Come on up." I gave him my apartment number and put the phone down—trying to think. I was too punchy to think of a damn thing. Except when the doorbell finally rang I wondered if Peggy's husband might not be coming for me with a gun.

The man was wiry and had a handsome thin face. His clothes said, softly, they cost a lot of money. In a way he reminded me of Matt and his Madison Avenue cut-ups, the same forced air of brightness; he was even sporting a brushed grey crew-cut which looked too young for his face, although he didn't seem much over 35 or so.

He stared at me and smiled, showing white even teeth. He said, "Now that we've looked each other over, shall we ring the bell and come out fighting?" He had a nice easy voice.

"Come on in, Mr. Preston."

He walked in, glanced around quickly, then took off his coat and sat down. I said, "I'll hang up your coat."

"I don't plan to stay long, Mr. Dolsan. Understand you're something in baseball. See you have a fine tan."

"I've been in Porto Rico."

"You and Willie Mays."

"Look, let's not make small talk. I don't think you came up for that. How is Peg ... your wife?"

"Upset. Yes, let us get to the point. This is rather an odd situation for me, or any man, to find himself in. You're the father of my boy." He didn't say it with anger: He seemed almost amused, as if we were both being oh-so-clever.

I didn't know exactly what to say. I kept still.

Preston rubbed his manicured hands together. "Of course when I married Peggy I knew she was pregnant. Up till now I didn't know who the man was. I didn't care and never expected to know. You've spoiled that—Peggy told me last night. She felt she had to."

"I didn't intend to spoil anything. I've been trying to do that well known 'right thing' but I've been clumsy. Let's get one thing straight—I'm not trying to hurt anybody, make any fuss. I'll do whatever you and Peggy wish."

"The last day has been a nightmare for Peggy. She has this horror of you appearing on the scene, like in a soap opera. You see from the start we decided the boy would never know he wasn't mine. It seemed a simple thing, till you came around. Perhaps you don't know much about these things but gossip, a slip of the tongue ... children, even grown men, have been known to lose their minds upon finding they were adopted, or one parent wasn't really a parent."

I said, "The last thing I want to do is cause the boy any harm. As I told your lawyer, I ..."

"That's what I'm talking about: Now one more person, Wagner, knows about it. Yesterday Peggy told him the situation because she thought she needed legal advice. Now he has convinced Peggy we should let you establish this trust fund. However I'm against the whole idea. Peggy is in a rather hysterical state but for the moment she agrees with me. With a trust fund in existence the boy will someday have to ask where it came from, why ... too many possible complications. Mr. Dolsan if you want to help the boy and Peggy, *our* boy, if you please, there's only one thing you can do."

"What?"

"Get out of New York City immediately and stay out!"

"Leave New York ...? I repeated.

"Leave now, tonight!"

"Wait up, I don't get this. Why should I leave town, Preston?"

"Should be obvious Mr. Dolsan. I've already mentioned the complications a trust fund might cause. As long as you know where we are, long as we are in the same city, in a month from now, a year, five years, you may get another yen to see the boy, start looking us up. Believe me, Peggy doesn't blame you for what happened—it was just one of those things—but you're still the last person she ever wants to see. I understand in your business you jump around the country a great deal. Why can't you leave town *tonight,* and stay away? If I may use the word, become lost, so lost that even if *we wanted* to contact you we couldn't or …"

The phone rang. I had a feeling it was another 'poison phone' call and didn't want to explode in front of Preston. As I answered it I put one finger over the receiver cradle, disconnecting the call. I went through the routine of saying hello a few times, then hung up, told Preston, "Wrong number or something. Look, you want me to take a powder but your lawyer agreed to ask about a …?"

"Mr. Dolsan, a lawyer looks at this from a legal angle, not from the heart. Perhaps he's more interested in the fee involved. Bluntly, Peg is so nervous she's on the verge of cracking and the only medicine she needs for her peace of mind is for you to disappear, never show up again. Dolsan, I can't afford to pull up stakes and take my family elsewhere, but you're single, on the go most of the time anyway. You can do it. Will you?"

I walked over to the terrace windows, looked out. I wanted to think. This Preston seemed like a decent enough guy and all I had to do was say yes and that would end things. Hell, there wasn't any reason why I should ever return to New York City again in life. Still if I could only make him understand, perhaps I could still give the boot to the old bitch. I kept telling myself it was more than just revenge, I wanted the kid to benefit from the dough. But I knew I was selling myself: The main idea was to put the screws on Mrs. Andrews.

I told him, "I'm willing to take a powder, but I want to see Peggy once, first."

His face got hard. "Can't you realize she's on the verge of …?"

"Listen to me, Preston, as I said I'm not out to hurt anybody. Okay, what's she afraid of? That you'll know? You already know. The way I see it, there's no reason the three of us can't sit down for a short talk."

"In Peg's state of mind you can't expect her to be reasonable." Preston's face seemed to completely relax, his eyes almost laughing at me as he suddenly sighed, asked, "Is it about the money you mentioned to Wagner?"

"Yes."

"I can take care of Peg and the boy, we don't need a few dollars from you, a handout."

"This isn't a handout. You said something about you couldn't afford to pick up stakes and move. I don't know how you're fixed, but certainly the boy can use money when he comes of age. And I'm not talking about a few bucks—I plan to make it at least ten grand, perhaps a lot more."

Preston stood up. "Won't that complicate things later on? We'll have to explain where the money came from, all that?"

"You'll have twenty-one years to think up a story. Look, let me talk to Peggy and if we can't work anything else out, I'll simply give her a check and she can use it as she sees fit."

"What do you mean by 'work anything else out'? What's there to work out?" he asked sharply.

"I only meant that the three of us would talk over the best way of doing it," I lied. "Tell Peggy to think of the boy's future: this is a money world."

"Once that's straightened out, you'll leave town and never try to find us again?"

"Right."

He put on his coat and hat. "I'll tell Peg, that's all I can do. I'll be back tomorrow morning, about ten. I'll try to bring Peggy.

THE SHORT NIGHT

Although I must warn you again, she's very upset and I won't risk her cracking up, money or no money."

"Talk it over, convince her."

"I'll do my best. See you in the morning."

We shook hands and he left. I read a book for awhile, thinking Preston was a good egg. I put the book down and wondered when Temple would get here. I felt fine about the small satisfaction I'd get from telling him I'd worked things out myself.

The phone rang. Was this another below-the-belt call? Had the old lady's detectives also found Peggy? I let it ring a few times before I answered. It was Peggy.

In an excited voice, the words still clipped, she asked, "Why can't you leave me alone?"

"As I told your husband, I merely want to talk about ..."

"My husband has told me about the money. I will never see you! I want nothing from you. We don't need your money. Leave me alone!" This last ended in a burst of hysterical crying as she hung up.

I felt pretty lousy, she certainly sounded like she was blowing her stack, as if I was torturing her.

While I was standing there, my hand still on the phone, it rang again. My busy-busy damn phone. It was Temple. "I have my car, Mr. Dolsan, and will be in front of your place in ten minutes. Be outside as it probably will be difficult to park. I've located Miss Fulton."

"You're too late. Her husband was just here and ..."

"Her husband? They're really roping you but good. Did he call you Ross or Dolsan?"

"Dolsan."

"Are you certain you didn't tell Mrs. Hemingway your right name?"

"Of course not. I spent the morning with her and made a point of not …"

"You went back there this morning? Goddamn it, I told you to ge to the movies! Be downstairs in ten minutes."

"Okay, take it slow and stop being the high pressure detective. Even if you've found Peggy she called me a few minutes ago, doesn't want to see me. She sounded hysterical and he said she's on the verge of a breakdown, so we'd better …"

"Dolsan you're a fool. I found her in a cemetery. Peggy Fulton is dead, has been dead for months. See you in ten minutes!"

His hanging up made the hollowest sound in the world.

CHAPTER SEVEN

TEMPLE had a year old Buick roadster and we drove across the 59th Street Bridge in silence till he asked, "What else did you tell Mrs. Hemingway today?"

"What do you mean, 'what else'? I didn't tell her a damn thing. As I told you, I was very careful not to give her my right name. We just talked. I simply felt like seeing somebody. I'd have gone nuts in a movie."

"Mrs. Hemingway must be a rather attractive woman."

"That's a real keen deduction," I said sarcastically to let him know I was annoyed at his smug attitude. "For the records, she isn't a beauty and she's dead broke."

"But things are looking up for the Hemingways. They've come upon a good thing—you."

"I don't know. This Preston—who you think must be Robert Hemingway—he seems like a good egg. And at no time did he ask for money. I'm the one that had to insist upon the dough."

"The best con men are the most subtle type. Dolsan, my first impression of you was of a guy who hangs on to a buck. How come you're so anxious to give away money?"

"Told you, I want to do the right thing by my kid," I said, lying smoothly. To change the subject I asked, "By the way, if you wanted a phone call traced, how would you go about it?"

"Your phone would have to be on a 24 hour tap and you'd have to work with the phone company—directly or indirectly. If you were doing it with the police it would be direct. If I was handling it, I'd have to pay off somebody in the phone office and it would be expensive. Even when everything is set, it's a difficult deal since you have to keep the conversation going for at least 20 minutes to corner the caller. Why do you ask?"

"No reason. Saw it done on a TV mystery show. Temple, are you certain Peggy is dead?"

He patted his breast pocket. "I have a record here that says she is. I figured her to be dead the moment you said the F.B.I. hadn't found her. Not that I think the Washington glamor boys are the wonders they're played up to be, but unless an alien is in trouble with the law—or dead—the last thing they'd forget would be to register."

"Do you know how she died?"

"Giving birth."

I didn't talk for a few minutes, then asked, "Did the baby live?"

"Yes."

"You know where the baby is?"

He gave me a long look. "Of course."

"Good." At first I felt sick at thought of Peggy dying giving birth to my kid, but the more I considered it the simpler it made things. With Peggy dead it should be a snap for me to take the boy, adopt him, or whatever the legal process would be. Not only would I make the old lady Andrews sore at my boy getting a half a million, but it would be easy to raise the kid—down in San Juan I could hire a good nurse to take care of him, a couple of nurses if necessary. No need to even think of marrying a Peggy now.

We were passing Hempstead and I asked, "Where are we going?"

"To a cemetery." He smiled: the dash-board light striking the planes of his thin face like a dim spotlight. "You hired me to find Peggy Fulton. If you will excuse a morbid joke, I'm delivering the body. Seriously, the cemetery will convince you I'm right about Miss Fulton's death."

It didn't make sense to me but I didn't ask any more questions. About twenty minutes later we parked outside a cemetery and Temple took a flash from the glove compartment. There was an old watchman at the gate and Temple spoke to him like a buddy, slipped him a bill, and he opened the gate. Temple and I walked through the intense quiet of the cemetery, the light from his flash bouncing ahead of us and making me a little jittery. We turned off the pebbled path, crossed some grass, and finally stopped before a small headstone set deep in the hard ground. Cut into the stone were the words:

RUTH   HEMINGWAY

1920   –   1957

I turned to Temple. "So what?"

"I thought you'd need a blueprint." He pulled an envelope out of his inside pocket. "Here's a photostat of the hospital death certificate of Ruth Hemingway. They could fake the age, and the height and weight didn't matter. But you'll see the concentration camp tattoo number under 'Distinguishing Marks'."

"Peggy was married to Hemingway?"

"No, no. Peggy was *never* married and Ruth Hemingway *never* died."

"Then ...? You've lost me."

"Remember I told you there are a number of ways of working a phony adoption," Temple said in a patient voice as though talking to a dope. "The birth certificate is the important gimmick in these greymarket deals. A simple way of securing one is to have the pregnant woman enter the hospital under the name of the woman who wants the child. In short, the Hemingways found out

Peggy was pregnant and didn't want the baby, so they arranged for Peggy to enter the hospital as Mrs. Robt. Hemingway, with the real Mr. Hemingway paying the bills and finally taking the child away. Unfortunately Peggy had a hard time, a premature birth, and died on the operating table. Well they had to bury a 'Mrs. Robert Hemingway'—they buried Peggy Fulton. The blind baby of the Hemingways, that's your child."

A *blind* baby. A grasscutter once took a bad bounce and smacked me in the groin—I had the same dull, sickening feeling in my gut right now. I mumbled, not really knowing what I was saying, "B-but you have only the tattoo on the death certificate to go on? Maybe the first Mrs. Hemingway was a refugee?" A *blind* baby!

"No, I don't have to check that, this fits perfectly. There never was a *second* Mrs. Hemingway. Listen: They hear about Peggy, perhaps through a doctor or a friend, or maybe they met her on the job. Except for Peggy dying things worked out, then you suddenly come on the scene asking about Peggy. That postal card scared hell out of them, they figure everything will come down around their heads, including jail time. So. Mrs. Hemingway calls and tries to scare you off by sounding like Peggy. But that doesn't work, you come to their house the next day and she gives you a cock and bull story about her husband being out of town. He phones you that afternoon, pretending he's a lawyer and gives you the rape scare, hints Peggy is married. That would have ended things, except you stupidly had to talk about money and they see a new angle. God knows what you told Mrs. Hemingway this afternoon, but you talked too much—as usual. Robert Hemingway drops in and puts on the act about his being Peggy's husband. Tomorrow he'll show up with a yarn about Peggy is sick, or something, but he'll take the ten grand for the baby. You leave town and they're safe—have ten thousand to boot. Be assured that from time to time in the future you would have heard from them; kid needs an operation, money for school … refined blackmail. You're lucky time has worked in our favor, tomorrow I'll nail him when he comes for the money."

He started to walk back and I stood in the darkness for a moment. He stopped, flashed his light on me. "Let's go, Mr. Dolsan. Be careful, you're crumpling the envelope," I had crushed it. I shoved it into my overcoat pocket. I was shivering, the cemetery suddenly seemed cold as a deep freeze.

"Nothing more to do here. I'll be at your apartment before nine tomorrow morning to take care of Mr. Hemingway."

"No … uh … we're not going to do that," I said, my voice sounding strange in the night, "I'll… pay off Preston-Hemingway—forget the whole mess."

"Mr. Dolsan, once you start paying, you'll never stop. What's the point in a pay off?"

"Well … since they have the kid, guess they could use the money. What I mean is, dough doesn't mean anything to me and … Temple, you know I can't stand any scandal, be the end of any job in baseball for me. I don't want to chance that." I couldn't stop my voice from shaking.

"I can arrange things so there will be little chance of publicity or …"

"Damn it, I don't want to arrest them!"

Temple walked over to me, his eyes bright, his mouth tight. "I thought it would work out like this. Dolsan when you first talked to me you were full of smug righteousness about doing 'right' for your kid. Even on the way here, you were anxious to know if the kid was alive when I told you Peggy was dead. You know the Hemingways' blind girl is yours but now you're willing to shell out to forget it, to be able to run away. Where's all your big talk now? You're ducking the baby because she's blind—I've met some frightful bastards in my time, but you top them all!"

I knew he was right as I swung on him. Everything I felt— the anger, the shame, the hurt—was all in that wallop. Temple dropped the flash as he ducked and then I was sailing through the dark air, hit the ground near the headstone with a thud that shook me to my toes.

It added: A little joker like Temple would be a judo man.

The flash was on the ground but still working, the light at right angles to us. Temple was grinning down at me. I took a couple of deep breaths to get the cobwebs out of my head, then climbed to my feet. I stepped over to Temple, feinted with my foot, then with my right, and belted him on the chin with a left hook. His feet shot out and he sat down hard, hands spread out, supporting his shaking body. "Just sit there and keep your hands in sight, Temple. I'm hell on wheels when it comes to stomping."

"Don't be around when I get up, Mr. Dolsan, or I'll have to hurt you."

"You won't hurt anybody. Judo depends upon surprise. Okay you surprised me—once. Sit still and answer some questions without sermons. I'm not paying you to preach."

"In the morning I shall return the balance of your retainer, minus one day's fee and expenses for ..."

"Why don't you throw that record away? Tell me, suppose I do want the baby, how would I go about it?"

"First we jump on the Hemingways, find out how deep they are in this mess. I'm sure we can pin an extortion rap on him, if he talks the way I expect him to in the morning. As for the baby, I think in time you'll be able to get her. It's complicated and I'm not certain of the legal ends at the moment. A father doesn't have any rights to an out of wedlock child, but with the mother dead I imagine ..."

"And while you're imagining the baby ends up in an institution if we play it your way—wonderful! And there will be headlines you can't stop. Perhaps the kid is better off where she is."

He grinned, a little blood on his lips. "That's one way of rationalizing things. You're correct about one angle, you aren't paying for my moral judgment. If you want, you can forget all about the kid and still not pay Preston—Hemingway a dime. After all, we have him over a barrel."

"Yeah, I suppose so. Anyway I don't have to decide things till the morning. Now get up before you stop being the only man in the cemetery with a virus *above* ground. And don't try no rough and tumble stuff, I'm in a nasty mood." I picked up the flash and we walked back to the gate and into his car.

We rode in silence and I kept wondering what the hell to do. One thing, I was impressed with Temple as a dick—in less than a day he'd found Peggy. We double-parked in front of the Towers and I decided to tell him about the old lady and the phone calls—I needed professional help. I said, "Let's talk for a few minutes. There's something else involved here, a personal angle, and I need your help."

"And your own kid isn't personal? Dolsan, happily I can afford to pick my clients and you ..."

"You know what you can pick. Stop shooting off your big mouth till you know everything about the case. I've been holding out on you," I said, and told him about the will and the phone calls—I even had to tell him about Doris and that was tough telling.

When I finished he shook his head, said softly, "I thought there had to be more to this—a half a million dollars more."

"I don't want the money. If I did I could have taken the will to court and had the dough. I'll be frank with you, I was never too sure I wanted the kid, and now—a blind kid. But I do want to get Mrs. Andrews."

"Isn't the fact the baby is blind more reason to take her?"

"Maybe. Maybe that's more reason too why the kid needs the dough. Right now the baby is in good hands. What I want you to do is find the dick making these calls, so I can pin it on the old bag."

"If you arrest her, assuming I can prove it, that would really make headlines."

"I didn't say I'd arrest her, I want to show her I know what she's up to."

"Be rather difficult proving anything. What makes you so sure she's hired a private investigator?"

"Told you, no one knows about Doris' suicide except Hanns and Mrs. Andrews. It has to be her, and since it's a man making the calls, it must be someone she's hired."

Temple shook his head. "First off, you talk so much it's hard to say who knows about ..."

"I don't talk about *that,* even to myself."

"And it would be almost impossible for your mother-in-law to know about Peggy Fulton."

"Well, she knows. Can you help me on this or not?"

"I don't know. Has Mrs. Andrews any other male relations around? Perhaps a brother, a nephew? Where's your wife's first husband?"

"I don't think the old witch has any other relations. Doris' first husband died years ago, the booze got to his brains. There's also a second one—Doris lost track of him. Can you help me, Temple?"

"I'll have to think about it. I suppose I could get into her house, somehow, plant a bug there. But that may not turn up a thing and it will be expensive."

"What's a bug?"

"Radio sending set about the size of a matchbox. Once in the house I pin it under a chair or behind a curtain. It will send for about a block and a half. I'd have to have two men, 12 hours each, listening in a car. All that costs. The set will operate on a flashlight battery for about 35 hours. You can see the difficulties—if she has a large house, we will have to install several bugs and during the 35 hours she may not say a thing we can use. And if she ever finds the transmitters and can prove we put them in— we're in trouble. We might avoid this by putting a tail on her, and on anybody visiting her. That's doubtful too, since if she has anybody working for her, he would probably report by phone. I could tap her phone, but that's risky. Let me think it over for tonight. Tomorrow I'll go out and see what sort of house she lives in. Before we start, are you willing to spend a couple of thousand for this?"

"You bet."

"All right. Now let's get several things straight—I can't guarantee results. What I mean is we might get a make on her in an hour and we might not get a damn thing within a week. If you should get another of these calls, and I think you will, try to provoke the caller, make him talk, get him angry. Either you might be able to recognize the voice then, or he'll make a slip that might help you place him. The immediate thing is what to do with Hemingway tomorrow. I suggest you stall him for a day or two, tell him you're going out of town on business. I also suggest you contact Mr. Hanns at once, get the legal aspects of all this. Of course I'm assuming you are going to take your child."

"I really don't know. Long as the kid—the girl—is well taken care of, and if she gets the dough … Ruth—Mrs. Hemingway seems very fond of her."

"Talk to Mr. Hanns. I'm sure you'll find you can't play both sides of the street. Let's get one thing settled, when Hemingway phones tomorrow you'll stall...."

"I don't remember if he's to phone or come up."

"Look Dolsan, this isn't any game, we can't afford to make a mistake. You talk to Hanns tonight, then call me and decide what you want to do. Before Hemingway sees you I want to rig up your place with mikes and a recorder, so we'll have him down on tape, be in a position to throw the fear of God into him. Unless we pin his ears back, you're in for blackmail. Will you get in touch with Mr. Hanns, then call me?"

"Yeah." I sat there a moment longer, then got out of the car. Upstairs I took off my shoes and socks, smoked a cigar. I couldn't think straight and the thought of spending the night alone had me spooked. I considered getting in touch with the call girl, Matt would know how, but I knew that wasn't what I wanted either, I'd still be alone. I figured a bath would help me think.

I took the phone into the bathroom and when I stripped I saw a bruise over my hip—the one point landing I'd made when Temple tossed me. I soaked in a hot tub for awhile but still felt restless.

I got Alva on the phone and told him what had happened, although not about Cathy being blind. When I asked, "Is there a way the kid can stay with this couple and still get the dough?" he told me, "Hardly. You might convince them to let you adopt her, but in view of all the hocus-pocus involved, it would be messy. I'm sure Mrs. Andrews would have a thorough investigation made. As I first told you, it would have been simple if you had found Miss Fulton, married her, and adopted the child. Even though you divorced her later, the child would still be your heir. This way, I don't see how you can avoid a scandal. You'd have to prove the present adoption illegal, then try to adopt the child yourself. I'm not sure a judge would give you the baby, and it would all certainly take a lot of time and make the papers. Speaking as your lawyer, I'd advise you to leave well enough alone—let Temple handle this Hemingway—is he related to the writer?"

"No! Okay, thanks Alva."

"Let me know what happens. And be careful. Let Temple handle things, he knows his way around."

"Guess he does." I hung up.

I got out of the tub and started towelling myself. I stared down at my legs—all the damn spike marks, the scars, the dead lines crossing my thighs—each of them had needed a brace of stitches. The clowns who had spiked me—all the guys I'd cut when running bases. I'd always played a hard game because it was my job, the only way I knew of getting someplace, away from the 'home'. I'd busted my gut and heart to get a decent life and now my kid … was she to go through worse crap than I'd known? And for what? I looked at the walls, stared at the ceiling—didn't want to see my legs, any part of myself.

I put on a robe. The quiet of the apartment made me jumpy. Turning on the radio I told myself to quit being a sentimental boob. I was giving the kid a fair shake. What had Ruth said, she loved the baby all the more because she was blind? What would I do with a kid? Ruth would take good care of her, and I had enough dough to make things smooth all the way. So to hell with the old bitch, no point ruining my life for some lousy revenge. That was the commonsense out: let Ruth keep the girl and my end would be to see she had money—give her my own hundred grand, if necessary.

I kept talking to myself, almost convincing me—except I was a bum salesman. Nothing changed the fact I was running out on my own child.

I couldn't stand hanging around the apartment, stewing in my own juices. It was late and I didn't know what I was going to do, but I had to get out. I was putting on my tie when the phone rang. It would be Temple wondering why I hadn't called back.

It was the same nasal voice that stood my hair on end. He said, "Les, you know why Peggy doesn't want to see you? She's afraid. She's very frightened. After all …"

Remembering what Temple told me, I shouted, "Why don't you have the guts to tell me all this to my face, you crummy son-of-a-bitch!"

There was a crazy laugh over the phone. "Because of the same reason Peggy doesn't want to see you. Even though you're driving her crazy, she has sense enough to wonder if Doris killed herself, or *did you murder her?* Did you hear, Les, I said *murder.*"

"What?" The word came out a scream.

"Hardly blame poor muddled Peggy from thinking that. Doris was ruining your career with her drinking, you wanted her out of the way. Might be convenient for Peggy to be out of the way too, although she isn't bothering you. But she can't help thinking that maybe when Doris was cold drunk you put her in the tub, slashed her wrists … Unless you leave Peggy alone, if you press her, she might think this aloud, to the papers…."

I dropped the phone, stiff with rage. I've been fighting mad plenty of times but only once before did I feel exactly like this. Once with Doris.

No matter how gassed Doris got she'd always remember on Saturday to buy an extra bottle to take care of Sunday when the stores were shut. She could forget to eat, dress, or take a bath, but she never forgot *that.* But this week-end she had lapped up Sunday's bottle Saturday night—by Sunday afternoon she was in torture with wanting a slug. It was the middle of one of our sad summers. I'd been tossed out of organized ball—again—for leaving the team in the locker room before a game: I got a call as I was getting into my uniform that Doris had been picked up on lower Broadway, her clothes torn and dirty, out on her feet, in about the fifth day of an acute binge. Hanns phoned to tell me she was in a bad way, didn't remember where she'd been or what she'd done and she had some sort of rash covering her thighs with scales. I flew back and took her out of Bellevue, to a ritzy private hospital on Central Park West that catered to juice-hounds.

They didn't claim to cure you, merely kept you off the streets while you tapered off. Doris came out three weeks later, looking fine, all the booze out of her system. We had a tender night where she swore she was off the stuff as she tried to show that booze hadn't drained her passion. Next to drinking Doris loved to drive so we jumped into the car and started driving—West. By the time we hit this tiny bluelaw town someplace in the middle of the USA, Doris was back to her fifth a day and I was sullen and angry and puzzled.

We'd rented a cottage, she was too high most of the time to be seen in a hotel. By Sunday afternoon I couldn't stand seeing her in pain—and wanting a shot badly *is* pain. I was afraid to leave her alone so we drove around, asking where a bottle could be bought. Of course all the bars were shut in this burg that passed for a town. After waving bucks at a counterman and a gas station guy, I found 'the place'—a chicken farm on the edge of town where a pint cost five bucks. There was a sloppy giant, all lumpy with muscle, running the place and after a lot of talk he agreed to sell us 'strangers' a pint. We were in his dirty kitchen and he brought a bottle up from the cellar. Doris had been sitting around in a daze but she came alive when she saw the bottle. Big boy took one look at her eyes, her grabbing hands, and held the pint over his head as he said, "Folks, it's fifteen bucks on Sundays." When I started to argue Doris cut me off with, "Red, pay him!"

Holding the bottle up like bait this goon laughs and says, "Up to three o'clock—it's twenty-five bucks after that and it's four now."

I guess it was the laugh that did it, and Doris in all her self-made pain. I got the same dull burning feeling in my guts I had now. I grabbed an empty milk bottle from the kitchen sink, smashed it, and rammed the jagged edge into his belly. I told him, "The lady needs a drink so invite her to have one for free—fast!"

His vest and shirt were cut, maybe his skin too, although he wasn't bleeding. His potato face was sickly pale and his knees danced—I'm sure we *both* knew I was mad enough to shove the bottle through his guts. He gave Doris the bottle. After a big gulp, when life and color returned to her face, she said, "Thank you Red, but let's not make a scene. Pay this grubbing scum." She walked out, the pint already hidden in her large handbag. I dropped a fin on the floor and followed her, the broken milk bottle still in my left hand. As I threw it away I heard the big ox rushing down the cellar steps. I started the car, wondering if he'd gone for a gun, but nothing happened. Perhaps he needed a pint himself.

I never forgot that afternoon because it was the only time I'd been mad enough to kill ... up to now.

I stared down at the phone as if it was a rattler and suddenly my anger grew cold. I bent down and picked up the phone, heard only a buzz. I put it back on the table, finished dressing.

I knew exactly what I wasn't going to do. Killing the old bag would be a favor and she'd laugh in Hell because of the jam I'd be in. This last call cinched it, it had to be her, no one else would have a mind crazy enough to even think I could have murdered Doris. Okay, so the hell with baseball or anything else, I was going to put the boots to the old bag by doing exactly what she didn't want me to do—get a half a million bucks for *my* kid. It

was time I stopped kidding myself, I'd learned a long time ago—
or should have learned—you can't run from the big things, you
can never run fast or far enough. Cathy was mine and whatever
I'd do would be because it was best for her—and that it would
also give Mrs. Andrews a boot in her fat ass helped this along.

And there was an easy way to do all this.

Downstairs I stopped a cab and gave the driver Ruth's
address. He was an old joker with a thick layer of fat over the
back of his neck and he looked unhappy at such a long haul but
didn't say anything.

Except for wondering if Bob Hemingway might be home and
what I'd do about it, I didn't think of anything during the hour
it took us to reach the end of the Bronx. I sat back, very relaxed,
watching the lights and the East River and the houses, as if seeing
New York for the last time, or the first time. I slipped the cabbie
a buck tip which should have made him feel better but he didn't
react one way or another.

Standing outside her door I could hear the typewriter
going—even though it was nearly midnight—the dead silence
when I rang the bell. She came to the door, asked, "Yes? Who is
it?"

"Les Dolsan, Ruth."

She opened the door a crack, then said, "Wait a second. I'm
undressed. I'll put on ..."

I pushed the door open, walked past her. She was wearing an
old-fashioned long nightgown and even though my mind wasn't
on it, I immediately noticed her good breasts had nothing to do
with any smart bra.

"It's rather late, Mr. Ross and I must ask you to ..."

"It's very late, much too late for that 'Mr. Ross' line," I said,
walking across the living room, turning on the light in the bedroom. Then I looked into the kitchen, and finally in Cathy's

room. I snapped on a wall light and Cathy was sleeping on her back in the crib. I stared down at her, don't know what I expected to feel—I didn't even feel much of anything.

Ruth had put on an old housecoat while I was touring the apartment and now she came into the kid's room, snapped the light off. "I don't want to wake her."

"Will it wake Cathy? I thought she couldn't see, or is that a lie too?"

"She can distinguish between darkness and light. You're most rude, Mr. Ross, barging in here in the middle of the night, walking through the apartment as if looking for somebody. I want you to leave, immediately."

"Let's skip the 'Mr. Ross' routine, you know my real name, you didn't bat an eye when I told you I was Les Dolsan a minute ago. And I am looking for somebody, Mr. Preston, otherwise known as your husband."

Walking back into the living room she still tried to carry it off. As I took off my coat she said, "I don't know if you're drunk or you consider this some kind of a gag. It certainly isn't a funny one! Now, Mr. Ross, or Dolsan, or whatever your name is, kindly take your coat and yourself the hell out of here!"

I had to smile at her with admiration. "I came up to tell you I found Peggy Fulton a few hours ago."

"You did? Where?" Her voice got rigid and a little shrill.

"Where else would she be but where you left her? In a cemetery."

Ruth's heavy face seemed to expand very slightly, then it went to pieces, a wild look in her eyes as she said hoarsely, "I won't let you take Cathy! I won't!" Her voice seemed ready to explode.

I clapped my hand over her open mouth. "Easy, Ruth, a scream might bring the cops. You sure don't want them around."

She started to cry.

"Look, you've already given me an act, don't add the sobbing-little-woman-routine. For a change, I want some straight talk from you."

She ran a sleeve over her wet face. "You don't have to talk so tough."

"How should I talk? Like Les the chump, the fall guy?"

"You were never a chump," Ruth said in a dead voice. "I visited Peggy every day during the month before she went to the hospital. She told me the little she knew about you. Not your name, but how it happened, how alone she was. The other night when I got the Special Delivery card I knew 'Frank Ross' could only be one man, Cathy's father. Bob found out your real name, I don't know how. I tried to get you to … to leave me alone by calling you, pretending I was Peggy. When you showed up the next day, at first I thought you were the F.B.I. and …"

"Looking for Peggy?"

She shook her head, a weary motion. "Looking for Bob. He'd been up that morning. It's hard to reach Bob but I'd called him at some of the places he … hangs out, the night before, to tell him about the card. He thought I'd played it smart calling you, that we'd seen the last of you. Then when you came up, when I studied your face I knew you were Cathy's father. Yesterday Bob called again and when I told him you'd been back, he decided he would see you, as Peggy's husband, try to get you to leave town and …"

"After he got some money."

Her eyes got big. "Oh no, Bob didn't ask you for money—did he?"

"Maybe I suggested it, but he's coming back tomorrow for it. Didn't he tell you about the money?"

"I haven't seen him since yesterday afternoon. Well you don't have to worry, there won't be any money."

"Did you also have someone keep phoning me that I was trying to make Peggy kill herself like … Doris, that's my wife, had done?"

"No. What do you think I am? All I did was try to keep Cathy. I have no reason to hurt you. Mr. Dolsan, you're a single man, you travel a lot, the baby was an accident as far as you're concerned. The point I'm making is you can't give her the love and care I can. You don't want her, I do!"

"Sure, you can give her all the comforts of life—batting out envelopes on a typewriter, while that ever-loving slob you call a husband plays the man about town."

"I can give her love, that's the most important thing." She sat down, crossed her legs. They were hairy, solid legs. "As for Bob, he's my problem. He's good—in his own way."

"Sure, he's a sterling character."

"Sit down, Mr. Dolsan, I want to talk to you. I want you to understand what Cathy means to me, how we got her. I said yesterday that you seemed an honest man to me, so I think you can understand."

I sat down opposite her. "Go ahead and talk, then I'll have some words. You may not lose Cathy."

She sat up straight. "I'll do anything you want—long as I keep Cathy! Tell me what you have in mind."

"You talk first," I said, and suddenly grinned. "We sound like a couple of kids. Look, I talked my guts out to you yesterday. You tell me what you have to say, then I have a proposition—it isn't any easy one or simple, but I think it's an out for both of us. Main thing, I have to know how you and Bob stand."

"It's hard to explain about us. Guess I'd best start from the beginning. And please don't stare at my legs. That's why I always wear slacks. Used to think when I was younger, the hair on my legs, along with my moustache, was the blight of my life."

"I'm a baldy, I like any kind of hair."

She smiled for the first time, that warm smile. "Let me tell you this as fast as I can, so I can hear what you have to say. To understand how I feel about Cathy, I'll have to go back to my own childhood. I was illegitimate, in plain vicious words. I was—am—a bastard. Far back as I can recall Mom and I were always living in a room, never a flat or an apartment, but a room. Mom was only 20 when she had me and her folks turned her out. She worked at anything she could get, maid, waitress. We were always hungry—poor. Mom kept me in the room all the time, she was afraid if I was on the streets, some social agency might take me away from her. So I was raised in a room, a number of rooms, all of them dingy, smelling of the last meal. When I was old enough to go to school I wore a key around my neck and right after school I came back to our room, read 'till Mom came home from work. My poor mother just lived for me, worked, scrimped, never thought of ever going out, perhaps getting married. I suppose the world frightened her and the only place she was comfortable in was the little world of our room."

"You sound like you disapprove of her."

"Mr. Dolsan, yesterday when you were talking about your wife—you kept reminding me of Mom. All the suffering you went through—the way you hung on to your wife, let her ruin your life, your baseball career. Why? Mom was like that and although I worshipped her, later I realized how wrong she was: You can't live your life for somebody else, or live some other person's life—each of us has to live his own life. Do you follow me?"

"I don't know."

"Perhaps I can't put it in words but I lived it, a kind of senseless circle: Mom lived for me and I lived for her—and neither of us were really living." She stopped to light a cigarette—a whole one. "I worked as a salesgirl during the day, went to business school at night, became a crack-jack secretary. By the time I was 20 I was making $50.00 a week. Mom was only 40 but already looked old, work-worn, troubled with a bad heart. All I wanted was to make up the hard years to her. We finally moved into an apartment of our own, bought furniture. I was 21, making $75.00 a week with overtime. I didn't want Mom to work anymore but she had no friends, no interests except me. I was in the same boat. I had no time for boyfriends, clothes, shows, everything was work, work, move to a better apartment, buy more things for Mom. Oh I enjoyed it, I was doing the 'right thing' by Mom. Does that sound too cynical?"

I shrugged, not knowing what to say, wondering where all this led to.

She blew out a large cloud of smoke. "Well, my mother died suddenly in January of 1941, her heart gave out. I nearly went out of my mind. I had a breakdown and spent several months in an institution. After I was released I found a good job but like Mom, I didn't know what to do with myself. I couldn't get out of the habit of working hard, but for what? In the summer of '42 I joined the WACS. It was the best thing I ever did. I found myself relaxed, at peace … in the army, ironical as it may sound."

"The old gag, you found a home in the army."

"It was so true in my case. Fighting Nazism gave me that old 'right thing' feeling, and all my little worries were washed away. I breezed through OCS, had my own company. I also became very much aware of men. I didn't have to be a beauty. I was surrounded by thousands of lonely men, not that I became a tramp. Anyway I went overseas in '44 and met Bob. Wasn't any romance then, we just met. You have to understand Bob."

"What's there to understand? He ran out on you, didn't he?"

"Yes—and no. Maybe it's more important to understand Bob than know about me, to get a complete picture of what Cathy means to me."

"Okay, what's his story?"

"Don't be so tough, Mr. Dolsan, it doesn't become you," she said coldly. "Or am I boring you?"

"You're still talking, go on."

"About Bob, the army was an escape for him too. He'd been married while in college, was working in her father's business, one of these deals where he was knocking himself out to prove he could make it on his own. They weren't happy and he was relieved when he was drafted. The war remade the both of us. When I was discharged in '46, I was far from the nervous wreck who had joined up in '42. I'd lived in Rome and Paris, had little money but a great deal of worldly confidence. I was 27, good jobs were for the asking, and I was eager to enjoy life. One day I walked into Bob in a 52nd Street restaurant. He'd been a tank sergeant, wounded twice, played a good game of crap, and had been discharged with medals and four thousand dollars. His wife was divorcing him. We got high that night and by the end of the week took a cold water flat together in the Village—only place we could find. The day after his divorce was final, we were married. It was fun at first, we were living it up as a couple of Village characters, and the name Hemingway didn't hurt. For a couple of years we suffered the mice and roaches and cold of the tenement, and the drunks and phony intellectuals—then we tried to 'settle down'."

She crushed her cigarette, stared at her slippers for a moment. "I knew Bob wasn't completely happy, never had been. He just couldn't get himself adjusted."

"Don't bring in the G.I. adjusting to civilian life angle, that's worn out."

She shrugged. "Trouble with Bob he never knew—or knows—what he wants out of life. We finally found a place in Staten Island and I enjoyed furnishing it, trying to know our neighbors and secretly looking down our noses at them for being dull TV bumpkins. We were settling down in the sense we were going at a slower pace. But Bob is always looking for something 'special'. He kept switching from job to job. One summer we both quit work and drove out to California, thought it would be different. We were back before September. I understood Bob—there should be more to life than working and eating so you can start working and eating all over again. Bob drifted but he always found good jobs: Manager, salesman, junior executive. Once he made six hundred dollars in a day at the track, and he even studied to be a TV actor under the G.I. Bill. He tried other things too—I know of at least one affair he had, but that didn't work for him either. I was on this baby kick, but Bob didn't care one way or the other. I felt we needed a child to hold us together. That was cockeyed: any marriage needing a child for an anchor is sunk already. When enough doctors told me I'd never have one, we decided to adopt a baby—and were turned down flat by every agency. I suppose that's the only reason Bob worked up any enthusiasm for adoption, it became a challenge to him. It was an awful mess of red tape; we were turned down because we're of different religions, because I was over 34, and a host of other stupid reasons."

"I don't get that. Must be lots of unwanted kids who can't find a home."

Ruth lit another cigarette as she shook her head. "That's the horrible part, the agencies don't offer *every* unwanted child up for adoption—only the children they're sure will be taken. Most of these agencies depend upon outside funds, philanthropic handouts, and they like to show a good record. They offered a 100 children for adoption and a 100 were placed—not mentioning anything about only offering a 100 out of the 200 kids needing homes. It's too complicated to go into now—the agencies have their side too. You have neurotic women who look upon a kid as an Aladdin's Lamp, mess up the child's life when he turns out to be only a child and not a miracle. Bob and I tried the greymarket but the prices were way above our means. Then one day Peggy Fulton took a part time job in a store Bob was managing. She was in her sixth month, broke … you know the rest."

"Yeah, I know. But if I'd really known I could have at least helped her with money."

Ruth smiled, a sad smile. "We gave Peggy $1500 before she entered the hospital. She wanted to leave New York and start life again in some other city after the baby was born. Cathy was premature-and Peggy died."

My guts got cold, the way I'd felt at the cemetery. "I feel as though I killed her."

"That's stupid talk, Mr. Dolsan. Nobody is to blame. Unless it's the whole world—for killing her parents in a concentration camp, setting Peggy adrift."

She puffed on her cigarette nervously and after a few seconds I asked, "Are you done talking?"

"Yes. But I want you to clearly understand one thing, I won't give up Cathy—no matter what I have to do."

"Okay, you don't have to give up Cathy. I want her, I mean I want to help her, but to do that, to keep the baby, you'll have to … to marry me."

Ruth sat up so hard she nearly fell off the chair. "Do you know what you're saying, Mr. Dolsan?"

"Yeah. Now listen to my speech. I believe you really love and want Cathy. She's my kid and I want to help her. There's something you don't know—if I have an heir she comes into a half a million bucks. All right, I don't have to draw pictures for you, a half a million will not only provide for Cathy, but in time may mean her seeing again. You'll be able to take her to the best doctors in the world. Now, in order for Cathy to be my heir I have to adopt her, and the easiest way to do that would be for you to marry me ..."

"But I'm married to Bob!"

I shook my head. "Are you? I have a death certificate which says Ruth Hemingway is legally dead. I don't want to get tough, but if I have to I'll put the screws on: Way I see it, neither you nor Bob are in a spot to do much arguing. I know you're 'dead' and Bob isn't going to make any fuss or ..."

"This is absolutely absurd!"

"Now wait till I'm finished. You marry me and I—we—adopt Cathy. Once she's in a position where she's entitled to the dough, we'll divorce and you can go back to your Bob. Although you two hardly seem to be lovey-dovey at the moment. I don't know exactly how we'll do this legally, but it can be done. And above all, I want Cathy to get that half a million."

"I can't even think of that much money, and it would certainly help her ... Mr. Dolsan—Les—there's other complications to this you don't know about. For one thing, Bob and I were married again, over in New Jersey, I switched my maiden name about. We did it so we'd have a marriage certificate when Cathy is ready to go to school."

"That doesn't change a thing. You've only been 'married' a few months, you'll get annulment or a divorce. Bob will have to do what I say. And if necessary I'll piece him off—a small piece of ..."

Cathy began to wail.

Ruth stood up. "She must need changing. And it's almost time for her bottle. Would you like to change your daughter?"

I followed her into the kid's room. Ruth snapped on the light and the baby stopped crying the moment Ruth's hand touched her, began peeling off the rubber pants. She gave the kid a rubber nipple to suck on while she put a towel under her and took off the diaper. The kid had messed herself up and Ruth folded the soiled diaper, wiped the baby, then handed the dirty things to me. "Might as well learn some of the joys of fatherhood. Throw this in the bathtub and let the hot water run on it. On the way back had me a fresh diaper from the pile on top of the dresser."

Holding it at arm's length I took the dirty diaper into the bathroom, dunked it in the toilet a few times to clear it off, then tossed it into the tub and ran the hot water, washing my hand at the same time.

"Done like an expert," Ruth said, walking behind me to get something from the medicine chest. "Sure you haven't been a poppa before?"

"I'm sure."

We went back to Cathy's room and Ruth sprinkled powder on the kid's behind as I handed her a diaper. The baby seemed to grunt with pleasure when the powder hit her, lay perfectly still as Ruth finished diapering her. Ruth grinned, almost proudly, as she said, "See what a good baby she is?"

"Yeah, let's get back to why I'm here. Tomorrow morning I'll take you down to see my lawyer, or maybe bring him up here and …"

"There's one thing I didn't tell you, Mr. Dolsan," Ruth said slowly. "I'm only telling you now because it's fair you know the sort of jam we're in, that you can get involved in too." She stopped, her wide face flushed and red. "Bob used my 'death certificate' to collect my $10,000 G.I. Insurance policy."

CHAPTER EIGHT

I STOPPED dead in my tracks. *"He did what?"*

"I kept up my army insurance. With a death certificate and Bob the beneficiary—I guess it was a matter of having the nerve to do it. Of course when I found out, I was so shocked we had an awful fight and I put him out—but it was already done. Every second I expect us to be tossed into the clink. That's why I nearly died when I first saw you, thought you were the law."

"I can see Bob isn't the lad to overlook an angle, but taking from Sam is strictly a rock play."

"I know it, but he was under a lot of pressure. Not that I'm defending him. Cathy left us flat broke, in hock and debt for every cent we could raise. We had about twenty-eight hundred dollars in the bank. As I told you half of that went to Peggy and she banked it—so it's lost. Then there was the business of moving—I couldn't suddenly have a baby. We had been looking around but Cathy's premature birth meant we had to move fast. Cost us $500 under the table to get this place. And hospital expenses—$16 a day while Cathy was in the incubator. Of course we had to pay for Peggy's burial."

"But to do such a dumb, crooked thing! Why didn't he go into bankruptcy, tell the bills to wait?"

"And chance people asking questions? No, we were in a squeeze, but we could have pulled out, in fact we just about made it. And don't call Bob a crook, he really isn't."

"What do you think Uncle Sam would call him, a dilly?"

"He's weak and … well, I told you I was the one pushing the adoption. Bob wasn't against it but when he found out Cathy was blind—it did something to him. All he could talk about was making a lot of money in a hurry—he'd sounded off like that before—but this time he meant it. He wanted the dough to fix her eyes, if possible. You see, in his own screwy way he thought he was doing all this for me."

"That's why you were addressing envelopes to eat?" I asked sharply and Cathy seemed to turn and look at me, then began whimpering.

"He offered me money but I wouldn't touch it. Naturally I've been thinking a lot about this. I know now that Bob and I were together the last few years because neither of us had enough energy to get out of a marriage rut that had become a kind of comfortable convenience. Would you like to hold your daughter, Les?"

"Okay. If you and Bob are on the skids, no reason why you shouldn't marry me, get the dough for Cathy."

"How can I think of anything but somehow clearing this mess with the government? I can't keep going with a jail sentence hanging over my head. I'd certainly go to jail along with Bob, and God knows what would happen to Cathy when everything came to light. Now, put one hand under her head and another under her rear. And be careful. Slowly walk around until she's asleep. I'll give her a bottle later."

I put my big hands under the baby and lifted her up to my chest, afraid I'd squeeze her too hard. Cathy kept sucking on the rubber nipple, not even aware of me. I walked around the room awkwardly as Ruth watched. I said, "This is still pretty simple. Obviously you can't return the money, tell the government you're still alive and it was all one big gag. Also, unless Bob gets into some kind of a jam, I see little chance of the government ever getting wise. Although if they ever do, they'll throw a real change-up: fraud, bigamy, maybe even a murder rap. All right, from where I'm standing it adds up to this: Bob has deserted you, in a few months you get a divorce or an annulment, you marry me, and he consents to our adopting Cathy. Hey, I think the kid is sleeping."

"You're a fast man in more ways than one," Ruth said, taking Cathy from me and placing the kid in the crib. She nodded toward the living room and turned out the light.

I said, "It will play—from what you've told me, Bob will probably be happy to get off the hook. And I'll grease him so that ..."

"You don't have to pay him off."

"Look, he thinks he's a sharp cookie but he's really small time. No, I'll give him ten grand so he can set himself up in whatever business he likes. You forget, if he ever gets in trouble, we all go down the drain."

"Let's not say 'we' so fast. Can you afford to give away ten thousand dollars?"

"Yeah, I have in the neighborhood of a hundred grand in the bank—don't worry, I really mean for Cathy to have the half a million."

She stared at me. "I've certainly never been in that neighborhood. What's it like to be rich?"

"I don't know, I never think about it. Even when Doris was alive, we usually lived on my salary. Her wants were small—a bottle every day. Funny, only time I was ever impressed with her dough was over a dime. We were in a hotel and I stopped to buy a magazine to read in bed. Doris said, 'The cover says they have a Dashiell Hammett story. I want to read him—buy *two* copies.' But to return to us, we'll spend the couple months it will take you to get a divorce down in San Juan. Maybe Brazil. It's not much of a baseball country but you and the kid would be safe, they don't have an extradition treaty with the USA. I'll see what Alva, that's my lawyer, thinks about it in the morning."

"Hadn't you best find out what I think? You're not buying more groceries, Les."

I walked around, stopped in front of her. "I still don't know what was wrong with buying you groceries. Can't tell, Ruth, we might even hit it off. After all, we're not kids looking for love, whatever that is. Frankly, I like you and I'm looking forward to the experiment."

"Sure of yourself, and of me, aren't you?"

I put my hands on her shoulders. "Ruth, you usually talk common sense, talk that way now. I know you'll do it because you don't have any choice. First there's the money for Cathy, that alone is all I need to hook you. Honey, you're way up the creek, so admit it. Hell, Bob has left you, way things are messed up you can never get married again. You told me about your mother, are you going to do a repeat performance with Cathy? No, let's face it, I'm your only exit."

She was staring right through me as she said, "That was about as blunt as it could be."

"Why should we kid each other? Are we in business?"

"That's the final touch—business! You know what all this makes me feel like?"

"Stop the big talk, make you feel any different if Bob was paying the freight? He's your husband but you haven't any use for each other. Come on, honey, we're about twenty years past the moonlight and roses stage. Will you go through with it?"

She suddenly laughed, high laughter but not hysterical. "Why this is better than any school girl's dream! In my 37th year, when I'm plump and hairy, and stoney, a man with a hundred thousand says he'll not only take me away from all this, but even give my daughter a half a million! Wouldn't I be absolutely insane not to take that?"

I shook her slightly. "One part of that story wasn't exactly accurate, it's *our* daughter. And she is, by birth and by death. Bob is coming up to see me in the morning, I'll straighten him out, then there's another matter I want to take …"

"What if Bob refuses? You don't know Bob."

"You're wrong, I've known a lot of Bobs. He won't refuse, I'm his exit too.… I have the modern snake oil cure—money. Now if we're going to play ball, this is how it will have to be: Soon as Bob's set, I'll talk to my lawyer, see what the first steps are toward a divorce. Also, best you and the kid move out of here—hide-out, in case they're ready to crack down on Bob. I'll know more of the answers when I come back here tomorrow afternoon. Only let's have one thing understood—from here on in we keep *all* our cards face up on the table. No more lying."

I let go of her and put on my coat. Here eyes were on me but her thoughts were miles away. She said softly, "This is all … so completely unreal, fantastic."

"No honey, it's real; it's the way the ball bounces. You relax and stay put till I come up tomorrow. If you want anything, phone me, only don't try to be Peggy this time." I pulled a couple of tens out of my pocket, shoved them into her hands.

"What's this for?"

"For you to stop typing those damn envelopes. I don't like you with tired eyes." As I opened the door I squeezed her hand. "Take care of Cathy. And don't start crying, it may not be so bad. If it doesn't play, it will only be for a year or so. I can see your eyes watering—no tears. By the way, why did you cry when I left here the first time?"

"I felt sorry for you. You looked so lonely and lost—and I had what you were looking for."

I squeezed her hand again. "Who knows, perhaps you still have what I'm looking for. See you tomorrow."

I took the elevator to the basement. It was 1:25 A.M. as I rang the super's bell. After a moment I heard his bare feet padding up to the door; an angry: "What you want so late?"

I said in Spanish, "Please pardon a friend who seeks a favor."

The door opened quickly. For a second his sleepy eyes were still puzzled, then they came awake as he said in Spanish, "Ah, the baseball man from Santurce! I will awake Olga and we shall have something to eat."

"No. I apologize for entering your house so late, but I will only be a minute. Would you be interested in both doing me a favor and also earning some money right now?"

"You are in my house, you have but to ask the favor."

I wrote my phone number on a slip of paper, then got three tens out of my wallet. I told him, "There is nothing wrong, you understand, but for certain reasons I wish you to phone me at this number if any time tonight or tomorrow you see Mrs. Hemingway going away. Not if she is only taking the child for a walk, but it looks like she is clearing out—phone me. And do not tell her or anyone else about this."

"But so much money is not necessary. I ..."

"Look upon this as a job."

He took the paper and the money, then hesitated. "There is no trouble for the poor woman?"

"None at all. On the contrary, this is only for her own good. I think things will soon be all right for her ... if you do not talk about it."

"Friend, I will not sleep, I will watch like an eagle."

"Take it easy, do not be too open about it. I shall see you late tomorrow. Remember, tell no one, not even your pretty wife—if you can avoid it. Good night and pardon me again for waking you."

I walked about two miles in the cold night air before I found a cab and I felt rather contented with myself. I had things under control, especially if Temple could pin those calls on the old witch. When I reached my apartment I felt so nicely tired I went to bed and dropped off at once.

The next thing I knew the phone was ringing. It was 9:15 A.M., the sun was out bright, and the desk was phoning to say a Mr. Preston was asking for me.

I said to send him up, ran to the john, worked a wash cloth over my face and armpits, and was putting on my shirt when Bob Hemingway rang the doorbell. Opening it I told him, "Just got up. Like a cup of coffee?"

"I don't mind," he said glancing around the apartment as he took off a light brown gabardine spring coat that must have cost plenty, showing a snappy rough tweed sport jacket that cost even more. The dark slacks and the white shirt and solid brown knitted tie didn't come from any bargain basement.

"You're a pretty sharp dresser."

"Never having seen you completely dressed, I can't return the compliment," he said casually. "But I think I told you before—in my business you have to keep up a front. These are my work clothes."

"Come into the kitchen, I'll put the coffee on." I didn't like him kidding me, figured I'd slow him down with a slap in the gut. "About your clothes, this front ... is that necessary for the insurance business?"

"I'm not in the insurance line."

I washed out the percolator. "I understand you are, specializing in the G.I. Type."

He was looking the kitchen over, maybe hunting for a bottle. He wasn't bad: His face turned a shade pale as he asked, "What are you talking about, Dolsan?" The muscles in his face didn't freeze, his voice didn't even shake.

"A clumsy hint, I know everything, as they used to say in the movies. I had a long talk with your wife last night." I put the coffee on, poured two glasses of orange juice and pushed one toward him. "Sit down and have breakfast with me, Bob."

"Bob?" he repeated, still playing it cool. "Peggy said nothing about having talked to you...."

"Come on now, the game is over—we're in the dressing room. I said I talked to your *wife*. You know the only way I can talk to Peggy would be through a crystal ball. By the way, I'm going to marry Ruth. I always marry the women who adopt my children." I was getting a charge out of haming it up, playing it cool myself. "Relax, Hemingway. Sit down. This is going to be another friendly session."

For a second his eyes got hard, then he said, "Sure I'll sit down. I'm a friendly character." He drank his juice calmly but his eyes were trying to decide if he could take me or not.

I went along with the gag, slowly finished my juice, reached over and put the toast on. I knew Temple would be sore, I hadn't called him, but it was too late for that now. And I could handle this okay.

The thick silence of the kitchen was broken only by the bubbling of the coffee. I'd goofed about one thing—I should have warned Ruth not to let Bob know about the half a million—we'd never get rid of him if he knew. He lit a cigarette and sat across the table, perfectly at ease. I decided to jab him again. "You sure made a rock play cashing in Ruth's policy. But she insists you're not a dumb crook, merely a mixed-up overgrown kid who ..."

That tore it. He snapped, "Ruth ...! What goes with you and Ruth? If this is a trap, I'll ...!"

"Can the stale music, Bob. Ruth had to tell me everything because a private dick I hired found Peggy's grave yesterday. I want my kid. Ruth and I think the best deal for Cathy would be for us to get married, after you divorce her. Then I can adopt the baby."

He was back on the cool kick again as he said, "My, my, you two seem to have made a lot of plans without consulting me." He pushed his pack of butts toward me. "Have one?"

I shook my head. "We could forget about you but we're consulting you now."

"Well, thanks!"

"Cut the hot air, Hemingway, there isn't much time. You may get away with this G.I. Swindle, and for Ruth's sake, I hope you do. But then again, Sam can nab you any second. The main point is, we have to work this out friendly-like. Guess you know Ruth wouldn't do anything to hurt you, although I don't know why she doesn't boot you out of her life for good."

"Ruth is a fine woman, the best. But all this is too fast, for a 'friend' like me. What is it I'm expected to do?"

"What you've been doing—stay away from Ruth. You two are at the end of the line anyway, so that won't be a strain. Ruth will start divorce proceedings on grounds of desertion, or which ever way my lawyer thinks best. I'm leveling with you, I'm only interested in what might happen to Cathy if the law fell on you. So Ruth and the kid are going to disappear, in case Sam does cuff you."

"A divorce might be risky, raise a lot of questions. Do you know we were married a second time?"

"Yeah, that's the marriage the divorce will be based on. We'll play it as close to the chest as we can, but there has to be a divorce because, as I said, the only way I can adopt my kid is to marry Ruth." I poured the coffee.

"Knowing Ruth, I believe she is willing to marry you—she'll do anything for that kid. Pass the sugar. I want to help Cathy, too. That's the reason I cashed in the policy, to do something about her eyes."

"What did the docs say?"

"I haven't seen a doctor—yet. First I wanted to run the ten thousand into something big. Fixing her eyes will require real money," he said, stirring his coffee, watching the ragged wisps of steam rising from the cup. "Hell, since you know this much, I might as well fill you in with all the details. I was doing it for myself too. I want out. I'd be free if they were provided for, if I could add a few zeros to the ten thousand."

"So you tried it and found out champ is more often spelt chump. The big boys took you like a dose of salts."

"No—not exactly. Playing the market and the races I had it up to nearly $16,000. A streak of bad luck has me down to $3,000 at the moment. But I'll get there. You in the service, Dolsan?"

"Yeah."

"Combat?"

"No."

He sipped his coffee as he said, "I saw a lot of action. I liked it, I love to gamble and combat was a daily game of high card for the biggest stakes a man has. Life was pretty wonderful, you didn't worry about a damn thing because there was always the big gamble tomorrow, or the next week. Tell you something, it was wonderful with Ruth too—for a time. But after awhile it got dull, full of boring petty things like alarm clocks and subway rushes and sales talks. I wanted to be on my own again. When I saw a chance of getting the insurance money ... I always thought myself a sharp operator if I had the opportunity."

"If you wanted out, why did you go through with this adoption deal?"

He rubbed his thin chin. "Why does a guy keep working like a slob all his life? Routine is a drug. I didn't want to hurt Ruth. She doesn't know it but one of the reasons the agencies turned us down was the fact she'd been in a mental institution, her nervous breakdown. That was punching low because Ruth is about the most stable person in the world. Got to be a kind of game with me, outsmarting those smug social workers. But with Cathy being blind—I couldn't take it. Another thing, we were up to our ass in debt. I still think cashing the G.I. policy is almost foolproof … Does this private dick of yours know about it?"

"No. You don't have to worry about him."

"I have to worry, I'm the one they will arrest. Only way I can get caught is if too many people know about it. Can't understand why Ruth told…."

The phone rang. I took the phone into the kitchen where I could keep an eye on Hemingway. It was some joker named Jim who insisted we'd played ball together with Obregon of the Pacific Coast League of Mexico. He wanted to tell me about a guy catching for a factory team out in San Diego.

I told him I was tied up, could he call tomorrow? He said he was only in town for the day, on his way back to California from a convention in Atlantic City. I said I was really sick as a dog and could he please mail me the info care of the Dodger office. He said he would—in a tone that said I could go to hell—and hung up.

Bob asked, "Was that the detective?"

"No. That was a lesson in how to lose my job."

"I understand you were quite a ball player. Too bad Doris ruined your career."

"What do you know about Doris?" I asked, my voice becoming a yell. "You son-of-a-bitch, have *you* been mak-those damn calls?"

He didn't have to answer, I saw it on his face. He was still seated as I swung on him. He went over backwards, unscrambled himself from the chair and stood up with the speed of a frightened cat. I came in and he stopped me with a left and right to the face that left me dizzy. I stepped in again, throwing a wild right, then let him have the business—a solid left hook to the guts. In slow motion he seemed to gasp and fold up—only there wasn't anything slow about the right he brought up from the floor as he went down.

It was a sucker punch and numbed the side of my head, then I was skidding across the kitchen, blacked out as I hit the stove.

I was only cold a few seconds. When I got the world in focus again he was sitting on the kitchen table, both hands still pressed to his gut. His face was screwed up with pain—except his eyes: They were watching me. Through his wide open gasping mouth he mumbled, "Don't get up ... Dolsan ...!" and damn if he didn't throw a snub-nosed gun on me!

He said slowly, still fighting for air, "This is a Webley Combat— better than our .45. You want to keep this friendly, fine. Otherwise ... I've used this before. You—you hit hard, can't be as old as you look."

My head was singing and the sides of my face seemed miles apart. I didn't try to talk, merely waited till my head was okay. I was mad enough to break his neck, gun or no gun. Crazy, thin guy like him able to belt like that.

He said, "Let's be sensible. I made those calls to frighten you off. I meant to hit a sore spot but I didn't think it would shake you so badly." He waved the gun at me. "Get up."

I got up slowly, my anger sinking to a slow boil. What the hell, he *had* only been trying to protect himself, and Ruth and Cathy, with the calls. I said, "Put that gun away. You're in enough trouble without packing a gun."

"I won this in a poker game during the war. It saved my life a couple of times. It may yet do me another favor."

"What's all that supposed to mean?" I asked, feeling my face. I wasn't cut.

"If it ever comes to a pinch, I have no intention of being taken alive. Serving time would drive me stark crazy."

"Stop talking like an idiot. Put the rod away."

"No. I'm not just talking, I mean it. I'll blow myself out of this world first. That's something I've decided for sure." He slipped the gun inside his belt. It didn't show the slightest bulge.

"How the hell did you ever know about Doris?" I had to say it twice, no words came out the first try.

"When she got your card, that Frank Ross bit, Ruth tried to get in touch with me. Naturally I'm constantly changing hotels—in case the F.B.I. was—is—after me. She finally reached me and I went up to see her early the next morning. Don't have to tell you that somebody snooping around frightened me silly. I though Ruth had played it smart by phoning you and pretending she was Peggy. But I had this feeling you still might be up, so I hung around the front of the house for awhile. When you came along I figured you for Ross. I listened outside our apartment door, too. When you left, I tailed you—damn near walked my legs off, and those big cab fares. I knew about all I wanted to by then and ..."

"How did you know about Doris?"

"That wasn't hard. I spent the entire afternoon following you. When you took a cab to the Hotel New Yorker bar, got stuck in traffic and walked the last couple of blocks, I was right behind you. Since you didn't know me, I took a chance and went in, sat in the booth behind. The Moores are a talkative couple. When you left, I joined them, buttered him up by asking if he hadn't been with the Yankees. Moore is a big fan of yours and while I fed him and his fat wife Scotch, they cried in their drinks over your lost career, told me about Doris. Hell, Moore even had a brief news clipping about Doris' killing herself in Canada, which he carried in his wallet. More I thought it over, phoning you about Doris seemed a finishing touch so...."

"Stop mentioning her name."

"I didn't know I was hitting *that* sore a spot. You sounded damn frightened over the phone, so I kept it up. Look at it from my angle, I had to stop you from snooping around."

"Okay, I see your angle, now forget it—for good." Everything was so damn mixed-up in my mind. The real reason I had wanted Cathy was to get even with the old bitch for the calls, and now it turned out she had nothing to do with it. Yet the odd part was, I didn't feel bad about taking Cathy, going to marry Ruth or ..."

The doorbell and the phone rang at the same time. I answered the phone. Temple said, "I thought you were going to call me before ...?"

"Hold on for a minute, somebody's at the door."

As I walked toward the door, Bob took out his gun again, said, "Remember what I said, I don't want anybody else knowing about the insurance thing."

"Think I want you to soil my carpet with your scatterbrains? Stop acting like something off a TV screen—put that damn thing away." I opened the door and Matt Blair stood there, on his way to the office.

He walked in saying, "Les, how about some fishing this afternoon?" He saw Hemingway, stopped, said, "Sorry, didn't know you had anybody here."

"Matt, this is Bob Moore. His ... uh ... son is a star high school pitcher."

Matt waved at Bob. "Sir, you're lucky to have the best scout in the business interested in your boy."

Bob was real smooth. "I know but we feel the kid should finish college before even thinking of a career in baseball."

"Follow Mr. Dolsan's advice, he won't give you a bum steer." Matt turned to me. "Surf casting would be a swell way of killing an afternoon."

"I can't make it, Matt. Busy-busy today. Perhaps some other time."

"Happens I'm free this afternoon—but … All right, some other day." He nodded at Bob and as I walked him to the door I asked. "How's your gut and the milk diet?"

"Pretty fair, Les. I had a good night's sleep and I feel on my toes." He whispered, "Isn't that fellow rather young to have a son old enough to play ball?"

"Must have married young."

Matt said he might play golf instead of fishing and left. I went back to the phone, told Temple, "Sorry I kept you waiting. About the matter you mentioned, that's been taken care of."

"I see," Temple said stiffly.

"Also the original matter has been taken care of."

"You mean you got the kid? You *are* taking her, aren't you?"

"Yeah, that's set."

"Did you get any more of those calls? I can start working …"

"That's over. I was wrong about who was making the calls."

"I see. I only worked one day, I shall return the balance of your retainer."

"That isn't necessary. Keep it. I'm more than satisfied with what you did."

"Is there somebody there with you?"

"Yes."

"Hemingway?"

"Yeah. But things are okay. I'm working out something."

"Are you in any trouble?"

"Of course not."

"Dolsan let me give you some last advice—for free. Don't pay any money to this Hemingway. From the little we know of him, it's obvious he's a blackmailer, once you get started he'll keep bleeding you. He and his wife will…."

"Everything has changed. As for the wife, I'm marrying her."

I enjoyed the shocked silence at the other end of the phone. Then, "Have you talked with Mr. Hanns yet?"

"I'm about to call him."

"About to …? My God, man, don't get involved in anything before you get his advice!"

"Temple, there's some things about this you don't know, and I can't tell you. But things have changed, I'm in the driver's seat. Everything is working out fine."

"All right, Dolsan, you're over 21, should know what you're doing. I'll put my check in the mail today."

"Told you that isn't necessary."

"I think it is."

"Well, you're over 21, too, do what you want. Thanks for all you've done and good-bye, Temple."

As I hung up Hemingway said, "I gather from that in-the-driver's-seat phrase you were talking about me, since you've got a saddle on me…. Who was that?"

"The detective I had on the case," I said, wondering what the hell Bob was talking about. "I have to make one more call, then we can do some talking." I phoned Hanns and made a date for lunch, then I got a cigar working, told Bob. "So you're Preston, and I guess you're also the lawyer—Wagner, or whatever his name was—over the phone."

He smiled. "Disguising one's voice on the phone is simple, especially for anybody with some acting experience. A handkerchief or tissue stuffed into the mouthpiece will do the trick."

"What were you working so hard at this for—to get your mitts on the trust fund dough I offered, like a sucker?"

"I don't care for the insinuation in your voice, Dolsan. Why shouldn't I work hard at this, as you so quaintly put it? I told you I'll do anything, even kill myself, rather than go to jail."

"And you don't give a fat damn about the trust fund?"

Bob smiled again. "It was pretty tempting. You won't believe this, but last night, as Peggy's husband, I was honestly trying to talk you *out* of any trust fund. That's why I wanted you to leave town at once, remove temptation from me. I realized taking your money would only complicate matters. But when you kept insisting...."

"Like a fool."

He held up his hands. "A fellow doesn't get ten thousand bucks pushed at him every day. Frankly, when I came here this morning I had a yarn set about Peggy wouldn't see you, but to make out the check in her name.... It wasn't a bad story and I have ways of cashing the check. But don't think it wasn't a struggle for me to make up my mind."

"I know, it left you pooped."

"Think what you wish. But my best judgment told me to scare you off and not have any strings like money around. On the other hand—you were holding out a soft touch. I thought I would really put the dough to work, still make something for Cathy."

"How? As a tin horn gambler?"

"I don't consider myself a 'tin horn' gambler. I'm usually pretty lucky and ..."

"I know, you were a hot shot crap player in the army. Wise up, the only successful gambler is a bookie, and he isn't gambling. Okay, if you had some dough, aside from being a sucker gambler, what would you do with it?"

He looked puzzled. "I don't get you?"

"Is there any kind of business you'd like to go into? Say in 'Frisco, New Orleans, Chicago?"

"What is this?"

"Look, I'm making you a proposition because if you every get picked up I'll lose Cathy in the mess. You said you lost most of the ten grand. Way I see it, if you don't have something to do, sooner or later you'll be broke and in some other kind of jam, and the government swindle will come to light. As a kind of protection for Cathy and Ruth, I'll set you up in some business."

"Are you joking?"

"Do I sound like I'm playing a game?"

"Well—no. You certainly don't dress like you're loaded."

"I'm not loaded. I'm straining to do this but I don't want the kid in a mess, ending up in an institution. And forget my clothes."

"I'm interested in clothes. I'm a damn good salesman and I have thought about opening a small swank haberdashery, like some of the shops on Madison Avenue that cater to the queers. I like handling good clothes."

"Could you do it for ten grand?"

"I think so."

"All right, once things are settled, you get the money and you open the shop as far from New York as possible. And we never want to see or hear from you again."

"That's rather decent of you but I'll have to talk this over with Ruth first. I want to make sure she's in favor of all this."

"Look, Hemingway, you're the one in a spot, not me, so don't give me terms and conditions. You walked out on Ruth and ..."

"I still have to talk to her. After all, I only have your word that she's agreed to marry you, the whole fantastic angle. She's still my wife."

"She's legally dead!"

"Dolsan, you're my guardian angel," he said with mild sarcasm, "I'm not fighting you. But I have to be certain Ruth understands what's happening. What's wrong with the three of us talking this over, making certain we don't leave any loopholes?"

What the hell, there wasn't any way I could keep him from seeing Ruth so I said, "Okay, we'll both go up to the Bronx together, settle this. This once, then you take a powder. Understand one thing, I'm playing this nice because I think it's the best way out for the kid. You cause me any trouble … I'll blow the loudest whistle you ever heard. Look, I have this luncheon date with my lawyer. Suppose you meet me here, downstairs, at three."

"I'll be here. You're right; none of us can afford or want any trouble. Meantime I'll talk to some men I used to work for, find out what the deal is in L.A. I think I could really make a go of a shop out there, sell the theatre people." He put on his coat and walked toward the door. "Three sharp, then, Dolsan."

"Yeah. And get rid of that gun, before it trips you."

He smiled, "Hard to part with a battle-buddy."

Soon as he shut the door I called Western Union and sent a wire to Ruth, telling her we'd be up by four and *not* to mention Cathy's money to Bob.

It was eleven-thirty and I had about an hour before seeing Alva. I felt like settling my slightly dizzy noggin with a long walk. The phone rang as I was putting on my overcoat and a fast burst of Spanish overwhelmed me. It took me a few seconds to realize this was the super of Ruth's house and he was telling me she just left the house with the baby in the carriage. I asked if she had a suitcase with her and he said she had a small suitcase and a large bundle of clothes in the carriage. I told him it was okay and thanked him, sat down and wondered what the hell to do.

I'd been a dummy not to tell the super to follow her, but maybe it would have been even dumber to involve him, get him suspicious. Only thing to do was call off lunch with Alva and take a cab to the Bronx.

The phone rang again as I was about to dial and I actually sighed with relief when it turned out to be Ruth. She said, "I'm out airing Cathy, getting all her things washed and dried. I thought I'd find out if you've seen Bob."

"He just left," I said and told her about the wire, asked, "Have you thought over what we talked about last night?"

"That's why I'm washing all her things. There wasn't much to think about, I hardly have any choice ... as you said."

"No, I guess you don't."

"Thanks. How did Bob take all this?"

"In his stride. He's going to open a man's shop in L.A."

"I can't believe he wanted money, that he ..."

"Ruth, it's best that way. I'm going to see my lawyer now, find out how we go about the divorce and stuff. Meanwhile you pack a few things. If you should see Bob before I come up, remember to keep quiet about the dough, also don't say anything about leaving."

"Can you bring up a copy of the will?"

"Why?" I asked, startled.

"Everything has a nightmare quality about it. It's not that I'm asking for proof.... Oh what I'm trying to say is, I want to be certain this is for Cathy's good, that she *really* will come into a fortune. Yes, I suppose I am asking for proof."

"That's okay, you have a right to see the will," I said, wanting to ask if she thought she could do better for the kid by typing envelopes. "I'll bring up a copy."

The operator cut in to ask for another nickel and Ruth said, "Then I'll see you at four, Mr. Dol ... Les."

"What's your number? I'll call you back."

"No, I have Cathy outside in the carriage. Frankly I only phoned to convince myself I hadn't dreamt last night, a ..." The operator's impersonal voice asked again for the damn jit. Ruth hung up with, "See you at four."

After phoning Hanns and telling his secretary to have him bring a copy of the will, I left the Towers and started walking downtown. The cold air was clean and fresh, like that well known tonic, and by the time I reached 34th Street I was ready to play a double-header. I bought an afternoon paper to see what had happened in the exhibition games, and took a cab to the restaurant. The driver's mother must have been frightened by a hot rod: we hurtled and raced and turned through traffic like a twister I once saw cutting across Kansas.

(In fact that ride was the start, as if my life suddenly took off from a ski slide. It seemed from the second I stepped into the cab I kept racing and racing, until the next three days sped by in one crazy blur of speed.)

At lunch Alva threw a fit. "Temple phoned you were doing something stupid, but this ...! My God, Red, don't you realize you've become an accessory to a crime—*a Federal crime?*"

"Maybe I have, but remember my kid is mixed up in this too. Now relax and give me some info about ..."

"I could be in trouble—disbarred, at least—for merely knowing about this and not reporting it! I sincerely mean this, Red: Forget you ever said a word to me about it. I'll certainly deny any knowledge of the crime. I don't want to ever hear a word about that G.I. insurance deal again!" Alva had been whispering and now he sort of sat erect, said almost loudly. "Now if you're asking my advice about securing a divorce or annulment from a recently married woman, and the adoption of her child, I can give you that advice."

"That's what I'm asking," I said, amused at the way lawyers think they can hide behind words.

"In view of certain matters—which I don't know about—I'd forget about an annulment. Since the husband is agreeable, get a divorce on grounds of desertion, but don't get it either in New York or New Jersey, somebody might stumble on the former marriages. Send her to Reno, where divorce is quick and routine. Also, might look better if you waited a month or so after the will is probated to start the divorce, and perhaps six months for the actual marriage. The adoption will take several more months. Make sure everything is done carefully—Mrs. Andrews' lawyers will certainly examine all proceedings. I think it's best you have another lawyer represent this Mrs. Hemingway. When the time comes I'll find one for you in Reno. Now about Mr. Hemingway, since you insist upon giving him ten thousand dollars, do it by cash, no witnesses, and absolutely nothing in writing. Make it very clear to him that he will neither contest the divorce or the adoption. And find out where he's going to live—you'll need to serve him papers when the divorce proceedings start. Red, this is risky as hell."

"Why? Suppose the old bitch's lawyers check—they find a marriage over in New Jersey, a legitimate death certificate for Bob's 'first' wife. Ruth used a phony name in the second marriage, that's the only thing they can trace, and that's almost impossible."

"Nothing is impossible where a half a million dollars is concerned. You're taking a chance."

"Guy takes a chance every morning when he gets out of bed."

When I left Hanns I took a cab to the bank and got the dough, then another taxi up to the Bronx. As we passed a small but modern hotel on the upper Westside, I stopped the cab and rented the best suite they had, a kind of modern three room apartment. I paid two weeks rent and registered as Mr. and Mrs. Lester Andrews, and baby, of Newark. The manager said they would certainly have a new crib put in. I started for the Bronx again and it was a quarter to three. I was on such a fast merry-go-round I forgot all about Bob. I paid the cabbie off and took another one to the Towers, picked up Bob.

He seemed to be going at top speed too—he was excited about a lead he had stumbled upon, exactly the type joint he wanted; a small but exclusive shop in Beverly Hills the owner had to sell because of a bum heart. He talked all the way up—about clothes, even had the plane schedules and said he was flying out that evening.

At Ruth's, things went into high gear at once, or at least the tension did, and it was all over in about a half hour. I again went into my story about wanting Cathy and marrying Ruth being the only way I could adopt the kid—with no mention of the half a million. Ruth quietly said she thought it was the best way to work things out. Bob agreed not to contest the divorce or adoption, said he only wanted to hear Ruth say she was in favor of things. I took out the ten grand—it was all in hundred buck bills and made a neat but damn imposing pile as I put it on the table. Bob's eyes got a trifle brighter at the sight of all the green but before he could pocket it, Ruth said she wanted to talk to him in private and they stepped into the kitchen.

I fooled around with Cathy, trying to get her to listen to my wrist watch. The kitchen door was shut and their voices were low and angry—but I heard most of what they were saying. Ruth was mad at Bob's taking the dough, accused him of holding me up. He kept trying to tell her it wasn't like that, I had insisted he take the dough, bubbled about his shop out in Beverly Hills. Finally in a weary voice Ruth said, "All right, take the money, and get out of my sight!"

They came out of the kitchen, her face flushed, his a little pale. He stuffed the dough into his pocket like it was soap coupons, slipped me the old firm handshake as he said he'd write in a couple of weeks, soon as the shop deal was settled; gave Ruth a brotherly kiss—and Bob was gone.

Like everything else that day, it was all very fast. I said, "See, that wasn't complicated. By the way, about the dough, he was telling the truth … I did kind of force it on him. Now, here's a copy of the will that you …"

"I don't want to see it."

"Why not?"

"I've been doing a great deal of thinking today, Mr.… Les. While it's true this has all been … unusual, I mean the sudden marriage proposal and … well, my attitude has not only been unusual, it's been a wrong one. I've been acting as if you were an intruder into my—our—privacy. In reality you have as much right to Cathy—perhaps more—than I have. You don't have to show me anything."

"Nuts, we're both in this together and we have to know the score," I said, showing her the will, telling her what Hanns said. I ended with, "While we're waiting, I think it's best you move, like we planned. I have this hotel set for the next few weeks. After that, you'll either go down to San Juan with me, or maybe go live in Reno for a couple months. We'll see."

"What about the lease on this apartment?"

"We'll pay it up in full."

"That seems like such a waste of money. In a few days I'll see the owner, perhaps I can settle the lease or sublet it."

She packed the kid's things and a small suitcase for herself. I dropped down to see my buddy, the super, and told him everything was okay and to forget about the Hemingways. Before dark we were in a cab going to the new apartment.

Ruth was impressed with the joint and said I was spending too much money and I said she was sounding like a wife already. We both laughed at the corn, and somehow it eased the tension. I wanted to send out for supper but Ruth said she'd rather cook, have to make Cathy's supper anyway. I went shopping and by eight we were eating supper and Ruth was wondering what would happen to the last load of food I bought—now in the refrigerator up in the Bronx apartment.

With Cathy asleep, we talked about finding a new baby doc in the neighborhood, then watched TV over a few beers, quietly talking about ourselves. At eleven I said I'd better be going, I'd be over first thing in the morning.

Riding back to the Towers I felt fine, it was one of the best evenings I'd had in years. I tried to figure out why, all we'd done was watched a few TV shows, most of them crummy, and gassed over some beers. Yet it had all been more ... more ... *friendly* than any of Blair's parties or anything I'd done in the last dozen years.

There was a note to call the Dodger front office. I slept like a top, phoned them in the morning. Some guy named Eddie—'Just tell old Red; Eddie called—he'll know me all right,' left a phone number for me. I phoned and it was another guy I'd evidently played ball with someplace who had a 'hot hunk of ivory' for me. After phoning Ruth I wouldn't be up till lunch I saw this clown and I did remember him—we'd once roomed together on a Kansas team barnstorming around the mid-west, playing sad ball.

I had to shoot the breeze with him, buy him a few drinks. He knew of a 'terrific' slugger who was wasting time in the Texas oil fields. On the way up to see Ruth and Cathy I phoned the info to the office, for whoever was covering that part of the country.

Ruth and I had lunch in the apartment and I stayed with the kid while she went back up to the Bronx to pick up more clothes. Cathy slept and everything went fine. Ruth not only brought some clothes but a suitcase full of the canned stuff I'd bought.

In the afternoon we took Cathy for a walk along the Drive and talked more about ourselves. There was a maid in the hotel who made a fuss over Cathy and I asked if she wanted to make some dough baby-sitting. That night, even though Ruth was nervous about leaving the kid, I took her to a movie and then for some Chinese food. Both the movie and the food were dull but I enjoyed the evening like a schoolboy's first night out.

Ruth kept phoning the baby-sitter but everything was okay and we got back in time to give Cathy her late bottle. When I started for the Towers Ruth walked me to the door, said, "Thanks for a nice evening, Les," and gave me that warm, big smile.

"You have a great smile."

"Including the moustache?"

I nodded. "Be okay if I kiss you?"

"Why not? As you once said, I don't have much choice."

I stepped back like I'd been hit. Said, "See you tomorrow," and opened the door.

She gently closed it, faced me. "Sorry I said that. I don't know, I was trying to be coy, or something as stupid. Of course we should kiss."

"Some other time."

"Don't you go coy, too," she said and pulled me to her. We kissed hard and hungrily, that big mouth strong and demanding. I was so used to whore's kisses I was a little shocked.

She pulled away, her face flushed. Her hand was on my shoulder and trembling a little. She looked me straight in the eyes as she said, "I've been thinking about you—I bet your body is hard and rough…. Since we're exploring marriage … I suppose we ought to see how we make out … there."

Her hand was really shaking and as I said, "Honey, stop talking." I closed both our lips with a kiss and her hands dug into my shoulders.

We made out very well—*there.*

CHAPTER NINE

GUESS the next two days were about the happiest I'd ever known. Ruth was just as happy. It wasn't that anything special happened, or that we suddenly found we were in love—although maybe we are. For me it was something I'd missed all my life—including most of the time I was with Doris—the companionship of a woman.

I don't know how to say it, but it was both of us sitting around the hotel apartment in our robes and joking about a TV show. It was walking Cathy in her carriage and suddenly finding out Ruth was interested in flying saucers too, and getting into a hot—but good natured—argument. It was being awakened in the middle of the night by Ruth's gentle fingers touching the spike scars on my legs and then her warm plump body telling me I was wanted in the best way a man can feel himself needed.

It was also small arguments, the rough edges being worn off as we got to really know each other, probed into the other's life. Mostly it was about Bob. Not that Ruth still cared for him, but she defended his little childishly stubborn acts she told me about. Why she hadn't chucked the guy long ago, I don't know. In a sense she was more like a mother to him than a wife, she always 'understood' him.

Like she was telling me of the time they drove out to California and somewhere in Arizona or New Mexico they picked up an old Indian hitch hiker. When they stopped at a roadside restaurant, the Indian was refused service. Bob got sore and finally a couple of burly cops roughed him up. Ruth talked them out of jailing Bob but that night when they were in a motel a hundred miles away, Bob suddenly got up, bought a rifle and started back to 'kill those bastards.' Ruth had to argue like hell to calm him down, and as she said, "It wasn't a grandstand play, he really meant it. When he makes up his mind to something like that—he means it. He would have killed those cops, no matter the consequences."

"I can see why he was sore ... but to kill—it don't add."

"Hard to explain, he hasn't much of a temper but ... it's something he learned during the war; once he gets himself worked up, in a mood he becomes like steel. I don't know in a way it must be a very satisfying feeling to give in to your anger—all the way. Of course I knew it was all cockeyed, but even as I talked him out of it, I had to feel a bit proud of him."

We talked about the little things in our past and the big things. I told her a lot about the places I'd played ball, the good breaks and all the lousy ones I'd had. How, before my legs went, I was fast enough to play so far down the baseline I could field most bunts for pop outs. Or if I got one on a bounce, still beat the runner to first. Like they tell me Prince Hal did, the great Hal Chase. It was kicks explaining the fine points of ball playing to her.

And the big things—I talked a lot about Doris, things I never told anybody but the head docs before, and Ruth would ask, "But why did you take it, Les? Why did you stick to her?"

And I couldn't answer, because to this day I still don't know why.

It was a change to lay on the bed and play with Cathy and the biggest bang was the time I was shaving and Ruth stood in the doorway watching me with big eyes. When I looked at her in the mirror and asked, "What are you thinking about?" she said, "I'm thinking I never want you to leave me, Les," and then we kissed and cried like a couple of jerky kids, laughed at my shaving soap on her face.

I called the Towers every day but not the Dodger office: For the first time in my life I didn't give a damn about baseball. The clerk at the Towers had the usual calls from old timers wanting to give me tips on young players. Those I could talk to on the phone I called back. Two persistent characters had been around to see me in person, didn't leave any message. I didn't tell the clerk where I was.

Hanns was trying to get in touch with me and when I called him he said, "Red, the more I've been thinking about your marrying this Hemingway woman, the less I like it. Especially if you're going after the money for the child. In one day Mr. Temple found out the truth, certainly Mrs. Andrews' lawyers will investigate and …"

"But don't forget, Temple knew about Peggy Fulton."

"True, but I still think it's very risky. They're bound to go over the divorce with a fine tooth comb, looking for flaws. I certainly would if I was representing the old lady. I'm afraid if they probe real deep, they'll uncover the whole mess. Perhaps you should forget about the half a million. It would be safer."

"I don't know, you may be right. I don't want anything that can break up my relation with Ruth."

"Is it going that well?"

"Even better."

"Then certainly forget the money—you have cash of your own—and it's about time you tasted some real happiness."

"As you said, we won't do anything for six or seven months. Then we'll see."

"Are you sure of her husband? Did you tell him about the will?"

"No. But we don't have to worry about Bob. I set him up in a store in L.A. He won't be any trouble."

"I hope not. Well Red, guess you'll be going south in a few days. Be sure to keep in touch with me. I expect the settlement of the will to come up for probate shortly. I'll let you know at your San Juan hotel when it goes through. Maybe we can have supper before you go."

"I guess so. Don't worry, Alva, I won't take a legal step without you."

The next morning I had to go back to the Towers, I needed some clothes. I got there after lunch and the clerk said the same two men had been around asking for me that morning. I called the Dodger office and they were kind of angry, they were sending me some info about another prospect one of their part-time scouts had found in Georgia, and when the hell was I going back to work?

I told them I'd be in San Juan by Saturday, then phoned a plane company for tickets for the three of us. I called Ruth and told her to get in touch with the owner of her apartment, tell him she wanted to move and see what settlement she could make, put her few things in storage, or whatever she wanted to do with them.

It was the first warm April day we'd had and I kept the terrace doors open as I packed, wondered if I should give up my apartment. There was little chance, or reason, why we'd ever return to New York.

The phone rang. Carlos Orta said, "My friend, Les, it is good to hear your voice. The season in the dress business has slowed down. I am out at the race track. You know my great love for a fast horse."

"How are you doing?"

"I have won a few dollars—at the moment. Les, I call for a reason. You remember I tell you about man who once stop me on street and ask about you? And you tell me to let you know if I ever see him again?"

"Yeah."

"He is at the track now. He buys many tickets at the hundred dollar window but I do not see him ever at the Win window. You wish to keep on following him?"

"Carlos, keep an eye on him. I'll take a cab right out to the track. In about an hour I will meet you—at the ten dollar Win window."

Downstairs the doorman got me a cab and the guy wasn't keen about going out to the track till I told him there was a five buck tip. I was curious more than anything else. All along I'd thought the man who had stopped Carlos after I'd talked to him, had been Bob. Now I wondered who he could be.

When I reached the track the 7th race was over and I didn't see Carlos. There were several $10 Win windows and I went from one to another, finally saw Carlos running toward me. "Les, the man leave in disgust after the 6th race. I follow him to gate and then I don't know what to do, wait for you or follow him. I see him take taxi and I come back here. Les, you wait here, I have horse in last race I bet. Caribe Brown—a hunch like that I must play. I return in few minutes."

"What did his guy look like?"

"Nice dressed, handsome man ... Les, the windows shut soon. I be right back at once."

As he dashed off a mild voice over my shoulder said, "You know what Bob Hemingway looks like."

I spun around to see Temple's sour puss grinning at me. He took out a notebook and read, "Mr. Hemingway dropped two thousand dollars in a floating crap game yesterday, he's lost at least fifteen hundred this afternoon and another eight hundred at the track two days ago. Three days ago he was in a sucker poker game at a Brooklyn hotel, they let him win $700 before taking him for $5,000." Temple pocketed the notebook.

"What are you tailing Bob for?" I asked so angry at the dumb slob I wasn't aware of what I was saying to Temple.

"For a client, and to work out the one day I owed you. I told Mr. Hanns I thought you were in a swindle, I know he won't mind my telling you; he hired me to keep an eye on Mr. Hemingway."

I felt sick—and mad. Bob the would-be gambler!

Temple read my thoughts. "It won't work. You can offer to set him up again and perhaps this time he'll actually go to L.A. and open the shop, but he'll keep gambling, and with the big boys. Sooner or later they'll have him in a corner and he'll have to ask you for dough. It will keep on like that."

Temple was right, only it would keep on *worse* than that— Bob would get mixed up with the law and somehow the G.I. insurance swindle would come to light and that would be the end of Ruth and Cathy.

I tried to think as the place came alive with the roar of the crowd as the last race ended. I asked Temple, "You know where Bob is staying?"

"He changes hotels every two days. At the moment he's living at the Wainsan, 45th Street, East of Times Square. He's under the name of Roamer. He ..."

I started to walk away, turned and told Temple, "Thanks for everything, and I hope this will be the last time I'll be saying that. There is one more favor you can do: The man I was talking to, the brown-skinned one with the busted nose, wait here a moment and when he returns, explain I had to run. Tell him I'll see him during the summer for fishing. He'll know what I mean. Thanks again and don't shadow Bob anymore. I'll get him in hand."

"Will you? How?" Temple asked coldly.

"Let me worry about it," I said, almost running for the gate, as people started to stream out of the track. I found a cab and told him to take me to Hotel Wainsan. The hackie was a young guy and as we drove off he asked, "What nag came in for you?"

"I never bet," I said, trying to think; my mind a blank.

The driver was a regular cowboy and made time, although he took a few side street turns to pad the meter. I almost wished he wasn't bringing me to Bob so fast—I didn't know what I was going to do when I saw him. One thing was for true—I was too happy with Ruth to let any jerk like Bob spoil things. I'd have to give him more dough to buy that damn store. And make sure he actually bought it this time by beating some sense into his thick head. I was mad enough to kill him but I'd have to settle for giving him the pasting of his life, make him understand I wasn't kidding around. It wouldn't be a pushover, he could wallop, but I figured I had more rough and tumble experience. I'd get that gun first, then belt him silly.

The Wainsan looked like a thousand other small hotels. As I gave the hackie a two buck tip he winked and whispered, "Maybe you know it, Mac, and maybe you don't—you're being followed."

"What?"

"It's a fact that's why I turned into a couple of dead streets, to make sure. A small black sedan was tailing us."

"Thanks," I said, looking up and down the busy street: It was full of cars.

"Looked like a squad car to me. Cops after you, Mac?"

"No. I have an over-zealous buddy." I'd have to tell Temple off and make that stick too.

It was after five and the lobby was fairly crowded. I didn't have to ask for Bob he was right in front of me, talking to the room clerk. Bob seemed sore about something. I could hear the clerk saying, "... I don't know where there's a game.... But I do know there isn't any in this hotel. We don't tolerate. ..." I was about a half a dozen feet from Bob's back when two solid built guys came along side of me, one on each side, and one of them asked, "Mr. Lester Dolsan?"

At the sound of my name Bob spun around. I said to the guy, "That's me," and I didn't have to ask who they were—they had dick written all over them.

The one who'd asked my name flashed his wallet, said, "We're from the F.B.I., we'd like to ask you some questions about a matter pertaining to the government."

I saw Bob's face go deadly white and I turned my back on him quickly as I said, "Why sure." There was a coffee shop at the end of the lobby. "Can we go in there and talk, or is this an arrest?"

"We only want to get some information from you, Mr. Dolsan. The coffee shop will be fine, if it isn't crowded."

"Great, although I don't know what you want of me," I said, walking them towards the shop as fast as I could, my legs doing a rubber dance.

We found an empty booth in the shop and I sat across from them. I was facing the door and the lobby, hoping I'd see Bob take a powder. We all ordered coffee. Somehow they reminded me of the sharp characters I saw at Blair's parties—they both looked like small town boys trying to make it in the city, wore the same kind of 'right' clothes.

When the waitress brought our coffee I asked, "What's this all about?" Trying to put a question in my voice.

One of them pulled out two photostats from his inside pocket and asked, "These checks were made out by you, weren't they, Mr. Dolsan?"

"Checks?" I repeated, still watching the lobby, and this time I didn't have to put any doubt in my voice. I looked at the photostats—they were a check for a hundred and another two hundred—both made out to cash. "Yeah, I made out these checks. So what?" I hoped the relief didn't show in my voice.

"You're a baseball scout, aren't you Mr. Dolsan, and you spend much time in Porto Rico?" the second one asked, a slight twang to his voice.

"That's right. Look fellows, come to the point."

"As you must have known, a number of Porto Rican nationalists have been indicated as subversives. Your checks showed up as part of funds put up for their bail."

"My checks?" Through the door I saw a bellboy running out of the lobby.

One of the men pulled out two more photostats. "This is the endorsement on each check, as you can see. Are you acquainted with the nationalists down in San Juan?"

"Look, it's my business to know a lot of people. I gave these checks to a … man … who gave me a tip on a kid baseball player down there." There was a lot of commotion in the lobby. The bellhop came back followed by two cops. The waitress stuck her head out of the coffee shop door. "That's all I know."

"A person like yourself, making constant trips between the island and the mainland, would be in an ideal spot to act as contact man for the various nationalistic groups."

"That's a lot of crap. I'm a baseball scout," I said. The waitress closed the door, said something to the counterman.

"Who did you give these checks to?"

"Some guy named Chico, I think, or maybe his name was Tito. I'm not sure. I met him on the street, he seemed to know me, gave me this tip and I gave him a hundred bucks. The rest, when he found out all the details for me." I called the waitress over. "What's happening outside? Saw some cops come rushing into the hotel?"

As one of the F.B.I. boys asked the name of the kid, the waitress said, "A man just committed suicide in the men's room. Shot himself in the head. I don't know, as the yak goes: People sure dying these days who never died before. Hear he was a good looking fellow too, as though we had them to spare."

I thanked her and one of the F.B.I. asked, "Mr. Dolsan, did you hear what I asked you?"

"Yeah. You asked me the name and address of the kid ballplayer I was tipped off about. Well no dice, that's why I paid the dough out, to keep the kid exclusive," I said, talking very calmly and hearing my voice as from a distance.

The crazy thing, I wasn't rattled or anything, and somehow I was sure it *had* to be Bob. As Ruth said, he had a one track mind on some things. He kept yapping he'd never be taken alive and when he saw the F.B.I. come down on me, only one thing made sense for Bob—*they were set to collar him any second.* I didn't feel sorry or happy about Bob's death, merely relieved. With Ruth a widow how simple things would be! No fuss or …

"Please, Mr. Dolsan, pay attention. This is the second time I've asked if you can help us track down the man who used your checks for bail money?"

This time I was really lost. "Bail? What bail?" I repeated like a dressmaker's dummy as I kept thinking over and over, with Bob dead—Ruth and I could be married *any* time we wanted.

The F.B.I. characters glanced at each other and the joker with the twang snapped, "This is hardly a matter to smile about, Mr. Dolsan!"

CHAPTER TEN

I T WAS a hell of a cold night, more like January then late April. The radio said it was cold all over the country—tough on the players who'd laid off all winter and were trying like hell to get into shape.

Alva was doing his conservative 35 per in his big Packard and ahead of us were the many colored lights of LaGuardia bright against the dull, cloudy dark sky. Alva was talking but I wasn't listening.

I missed Ruth already and I'd left her a half hour ago. She and Cathy were coming to San Juan next week. Bob's death had broken her up but she was okay now, had to stay behind to bury him and settle the apartment. We'd been lucky, there hadn't been much fuss about his suicide—a column in the next day's papers and that was all. People in the house had told the reporters Bob had separated from his wife and the story tone had been about the unhappy husband still upset over his former wife's death. It couldn't have fitted better if we had planned it.

Alva nudged me. "Red, are you sleeping?"

"No. I heard you, you told the F.B.I. off."

"I certainly did. Why in all my 36 years in law I never heard it was a crime to put up bail. Not that you did, but even if you had, they had no right to badger you."

"Guess they got a little nasty because I wouldn't tell them who I gave the check to. Hell with that, it's over. Don't forget Alva, I told Ruth to call you if she needs any help."

"Of course. I want to talk about Ruth. In view of the unfortunate death of her husband, I'd advise you to wait a proper time, say six months, before marrying her. Cathy's adoption will be a simple court matter. Mr. Hemingway's death changes my opinion about seeking the half a million. You are marrying a widow with a child. Mrs. Andrews' lawyers will still check, of course, but in my opinion there's very little chance they'll find any irregularities. This is far different than a divorce. So now I advise you to go ahead with your plans. A few months after you are married, I'll start the adoption proceedings. I believe that some time next year we will be able to inform Mrs. Andrews you have an heir."

"If she knew about things now, she'd probably wreck the plane to knock me off before I can marry Ruth."

"Red, you have a morbid sense of humor—if it can be called either sense or humor. There is one more matter I wish to advise you on—off the record," he said as we turned into the airport driveway. "Under no circumstances are you to suddenly get any rightous ideas about ever returning the ten thousand dollars Mr. Hemingway … eh … swindled, to the government. While it would be the moral thing to do, it would certainly start a million questions that …"

"Ruth and I have already got that licked. We're evening matters up by *not* collecting Bob's policy."

"What's this Bob's policy?"

"Bob kept up his $10,000 G.I. policy too. We've decided to forget about it, not make any claim. That will sort of pay us up with Sam, at least in our own minds. Anything else?"

Alva seemed deep in thought as he parked the car, then he said, "I think we've covered things. I believe you're pretty well in the clear."

"I know I am," I said, getting out, yanking my old pigskin bag off the back seat. I looked around like a hick as we walked into the terminal building. A lot had happened in the two weeks since I landed here. Now I liked the lights, the rushing people, all the action. Now I was a part of it because for the first time an airport didn't seem cold and lonely to me.

I greeted it like an old friend, like a guy who has it made for sure.

THE END.